D0500178

BEFORE THEY MAKE YOU RUN

OTHER FIVE STAR TITLES BY JAMES PATRICK HUNT

Hunt, James Patrick, 196
Before they make you
run /
2006.
33305211669571
sa   03/23/07

BEFORE THEY MAKE YOU RUN

JAMES PATRICK HUNT

FIVE STAR

An imprint of Thomson Gale, a part of The Thomson Corporation

THOMSON

GALE

Detroit • New York • San Francisco • New Haven, Conn. • Waterville, Maine • London

Copyright © 2006 by James Patrick Hunt
Thomson Gale is part of The Thomson Corporation.
Thomson and Star Logo and Five Star are trademarks and Gale is a registered trademark used herein under license.

ALL RIGHTS RESERVED
This novel is a work of fiction. Names, characters, places and incidents are either the product of the author's imagination, or, if real, used fictitiously.
No part of this book may be reproduced or transmitted in any form or by any electronic or mechanical means, including photocopying, recording or by any information storage and retrieval system, without the express written permission of the publisher, except where permitted by law.
Set in 11 pt. Plantin.

LIBRARY OF CONGRESS CATALOGING-IN-PUBLICATION DATA

Hunt, James Patrick, 1964–
    Before they make you run / James Patrick Hunt.—1st ed.
    p. cm.
    ISBN 1-59414-427-3 (alk. paper)
    1. Lawyers—Fiction. 2. Judges—Fiction. 3. Police corruption—Fiction.
I. Title.
PS3608.U577B45 2006
813'.6—dc22   2006018302

U.S. Hardcover:
ISBN 13: 978-1-59414-427-1
ISBN 10: 1-59414-427-3

First Edition. First Printing: October 2006.

Published in 2006 in conjunction with Tekno Books and Ed Gorman.

Printed in the United States of America on permanent paper
10 9 8 7 6 5 4 3 2 1

"I've never had a problem with drugs, only with policemen."

—Keith Richards

For Aunt Fran and Aunt Nancy

ONE

Van said, "Slow down."

Officer Buddy Matlock eased off the accelerator, bringing the Crown Victoria felony car down to seventy-five.

"Sixty-five, Buddy." Van said, "We're not in Oklahoma anymore. Speed limit's lower here."

"Sorry, Van." Buddy said, "I just figured . . . well, we are cops."

Sitting in the front passenger seat, Van turned to look at Buddy and saw . . . what? Big, dumbass redneck fool. A good boy, but a boy. He needed guidance.

Van said, "We're not in a marked car. We get pulled over by highway patrol, they'll see our uniforms and ask us what we're doing in their territory and then they'll know. But then they'll want to shoot the shit for a while, talk shop, and we'll be late. You know highway patrol."

Buddy didn't pick up on it, so Van helped him out.

"They get bored," Van said. "Christ, I'd get bored too if I had to drive up and down highways for an eight-hour shift. Talking to us may be the highlight of their day."

Buddy nodded his head, pretending to remember something he had already known. Ah, of course. Highway patrol.

In the back seat, Officer Ray Miller said, "They're proud sonsabitches, though. Hear them tell it, being in highway patrol is like being a goddamn Navy Seal. Every trooper I ever met, acted like he was a member of some sort of Praetorian Guard.

All they're fucking doing is giving speeding tickets."

"Well," Buddy said, "they do guard the governor."

"What," Ray said, "like two of 'em? And they're basically just chauffeurs. I'm not saying they're bad guys or nothing, but it ain't police work."

Van did not agree with this generalization. He was a patrol lieutenant in the Tulsa Police Department. He took pride in patrol, pride in the uniform. But he didn't want to get involved in the conversation so he let Buddy and Ray continue between themselves. He felt better now that Buddy had brought the speed down. Buddy. Remembering they were cops, but forgetting that a cop had to use a certain amount of discretion when stretching the law. A time to ignore, a time to abide, a time to live and prosper, and a time to watch your ass. There were days you could relax, kill forty-five minutes telling war stories with a Missouri cop. Other days, you had to be careful and stick to the plan.

This was one of those stick-to-the-plan days.

A woman had once told Van that he looked like a young Kris Kristofferson. Not lately; no, back when he was handsome and did all those movies in the seventies: *Alice Doesn't Live Here Anymore, Blume in Love, Pat Garrett and Billy the Kid.* Van had never seen any of those. But he told the woman he had seen *Semi-Tough* and had she seen that one? "Yeah, yeah," she said. "That is *so* you." With the long hair and the mustache and that total, laid-back coolness. Very sexy, she said. Van liked hearing that. He remembered the part where Kristofferson talked Brian Dennehy out of dropping a girl off the top of a house. Standing next to the shaved bear as he dangled the screaming girl by her ankles, scaring the devil out of the poor thing and everyone down below. Not pleading with Dennehy, but just talking to him, smooth and cool, laughing and smiling, controlling the bigger, more violent man, controlling the situation. Yeah, Van could relate to that.

He was forty-two years old, still in good shape. Flat stomach, thick brown hair worn longish, longer than regulation length, healthy sideburns and 'stash. He looked good in the uniform.

He joined the Tulsa Police Department when he was twenty-one, after two years in junior college. He liked to tell people he just fell into it, that he went with a buddy to take the entrance exam because he had nothing else to do that day. But that wasn't really true. He had always wanted to be a cop. Like a lot of men in the profession, he was drawn to the power and the authority of the job. He was drawn to the club. He rose in the ranks fairly quickly, using whatever means necessary, and became a patrol lieutenant in his early thirties.

He was a natural leader of men. But, in part, he credited his success on his ability to see the big picture. Greg Vannerson considered himself something of a philosopher and he felt he understood a cop's nature better than most. He knew that the typical police officer was attracted to authority. And that this attraction was both a strength and a weakness. That is, he believed that that attraction cut two ways: the authority the police officer coveted was also the authority he feared. It was this nameless Authority that the cop served and protected. Not the public. The cop who placed himself in this role of Authority—who *seeks* to place himself in this role—gave Authority more credit than it deserved, and accordingly, feared it more than he should. In Van's experience, the typical cop would fall apart during the internal affairs (IA) investigation, go all Catholic with the confessions, and rat out his own partner if he got scared enough, and almost all of them did. He'd make a low-level drug dealer give it up on Monday, then give it up himself to IA on Wednesday. The lone wolf who bucks the system and tells his tight-assed superior officer to shove it, man, because he's got a job to do . . . the guy played by Clint Eastwood, Bruce Willis, or Nick Nolte in any one of a hundred movies and yet never seems to get fired for insubordination or dereliction of duty . . . well, you weren't going to find that guy at your local police headquarters. This maverick was a pure Hollywood creation. If he was the sort of guy that resented authority, he wouldn't have *become* a policeman. He certainly wouldn't remain one for very long.

As Van saw it, the key to it all was to use the capital "A" authority when you needed it, but not to go apeshit when it was pounding on your door. The key was to make it work for you, and only for you. Play the game, nod your head with a serious expression when the occasion called for it, go home, shut your door, and laugh at the fools who think they're running things.

Yet, so few cops had figured it out. Dipshits, most of them. But that was fine with Van. It was better to be one of the few who understood.

Van would think these things through, when he had a lot of time on his hands. He was not afraid to think. He liked to use the downtime to his advantage, relax his mind. Like now . . . riding shotgun in a maroon Tulsa PD Crown Victoria, somewhere in the show-me state of Missouri on I-44.

Next to him, driving the felony car, was Officer Buddy Matlock. A big man, six-foot-three, broad-shouldered, the beginnings of a paunch hanging over his belt. Hair cut short, starting to gray at the temples. When he smiled, he displayed a good set of teeth, even and white. But it was a cold smile, and those teeth usually prompted fear when bared. Buddy would flash the smile at women after pulling them over for going two miles over the speed limit. He would lean into the driver's side window and say, "Where's a sweet lady like yourself got to hurry to?" He would touch them on the shoulder. He would write his cell number on the back of his card, hand it to them and say, "Now I don't give this number out to just anyone. I want you to call me sometime." He never gave out his home number; he was married with three children. Once in a while a woman would call him. Most of them didn't. A couple of women called the police station instead to file complaints against the scary cop who was coming on to them. The complaints never amounted to anything.

One of them reported that she did agree to meet Buddy for drinks, but that when she did, she suddenly got creeped out and tried to leave. That Buddy caught up with her in the parking lot, grabbed her, and forced himself on her. That he tried to tear her blouse off. That he slapped her when she resisted. That the only thing that stopped him from raping her was the approaching headlights of a car.

After he was notified of the pending investigation, big Buddy Matlock came to Van in tears, saying, "What am I gonna do? What am I gonna do?" Panicking, the dumbshit. Greg Vannerson told him, above all, calm down, will you? They saw him blubbering like this they'd know he tried to rape the broad. Van told him that everything would be fine so long as he resisted his stupid cop's urge to confess. Just keep quiet, lie low, and let Uncle Greg take care of it.

He did, too. Lt. Vannerson got himself appointed to the investigation panel with the two other officers. The officers were, of course, junior in rank to him, and one of them had once been bailed out by Van himself. Van made a show of reviewing the woman's written statement and witness testimony, let the others see that he was being thoughtful, not wanting to rush to judgment. He took his time laying the foundation for clearance.

First, he pointed out that the complainant was a barmaid with a record who couldn't hold a job. That she didn't have custody of her own kid. Then he noted all the inconsistencies of the woman's story, glossing over the fact that a lot of her assertions were merely inconsistent with Buddy's version of the events. He reminded the panel that the lady herself admitted she'd had a lot to drink. And then he reminded them that Buddy was a family man, and there were was no physical proof of assault. He warned the panel that the woman was simply trying to find a way to create a lawsuit against the police department, that she was another one of these people who just hates cops. What she really wanted was to come after all of them, and they shouldn't be helping her do it.

The investigation panel declined to recommend disciplinary investigation. No complaint was ever forwarded to the District Attorney's Office.

In the back seat was Officer Ray Miller. He was physically smaller than Buddy Matlock, around six feet and weighing one-eighty. He came from Lane, a small, impoverished town in the southeastern part of the state. He wore his dark hair in a crewcut. He had joined the force three years ago, after he mustered out of the Navy. He felt lucky to have gotten on with the Tulsa police; they paid almost three times better than any job he could have found in the southeast Piney Woods. He had met up with Greg Vannerson almost immediately. Greg invited him to Cassy's for what he called "happy times." It was there that Ray met the first really good-looking girl he'd banged. Young thing named Sandy McGuire with large breasts and shiny skin. Lined up by Greg. She was a whore, of course. But then, he hadn't paid for it. Greg had. Or someone had. So maybe it wasn't like being with a whore. In any event, Ray didn't complain.

In his rookie year, Ray drove his patrol car to Dub Richardson Ford to test drive one of their new Mustang 5.0's. He got it up to 147 mph on the Broken Arrow expressway and tried to bank off the 15th Street exit and lost it. The car turned over six times before coming to a rest. His partner spent three weeks in the hospital.

Ray's sergeant told him termination was a guarantee. Man, he was lucky he wasn't getting arrested for involuntary infliction of serious bodily harm. Ray believed him; he saw himself returning to the hopelessness and poverty of southeast Oklahoma, hat in hand. But Greg Vannerson came to him and before Ray could even say anything, Van said, "Why didn't you come to me?" Like his feelings were hurt. Van said he would see what he could do.

Van sat on that investigation panel too. Before the panel, Van said he hated to say it, but the man who was truly at fault lay in a hospital bed at Tulsa Regional. That guy was Ray Miller's senior partner; he had six years seniority on this poor kid from southeast Oklahoma. *He* should have known better. He should've said, hey, dumbass, we're not going to race this Mustang on duty. Instead, he rode along and *encouraged* the young whippersnapper. If senior officers like us couldn't be trusted to set a good example for the young guys, weren't we the ones who were to blame? At most, the young hick from Little Dixie deserved ten days on the ground.

So the panel gave Ray Miller ten days' suspension without pay.

The panel never did learn about Ray Miller's other offenses. They never learned about the time Ray chased down a teenager named Ronnie Cremers, who had been driving a Honda Civic and decided to run away for a while for shits and giggles, while this Tulsa cop chased him. He stopped on the south side and put his arms out the window to surrender. But Officer Ray Miller wasn't interested in that anymore. He pulled Ronnie Cremers out, threw him on the pavement and kicked him in the ribs and head until his partner (his second one) pulled him away, yelling, "Chill, man, chill!"

Ronnie Cremers survived the beating. At the hospital, he received a visit from Lt. Vannerson who told him that though Officer Miller tended to get overly excited sometimes, there were some very serious criminal violations Ronnie himself had committed. These charges were not just limited to reckless driving, but also included possession of cocaine with intent to distribute.

Ronnie said, "Cocaine?"

Yes, sir. They had found a bag stuffed into his console that had a street value of at least $15,000. A five-year minimum under the federal guidelines.

Ronnie Cremers lay in his hospital bed, staring at the mustached cop. He knew it would be no use telling the cop he had never even tried cocaine let alone tried to sell it. No use telling the cop he was just a simpleminded drunk who wanted to be in a car chase and ended up almost getting killed by some nutjob cop. He knew this cop who never said his name had put the cocaine in his car, or had someone else do it. He knew this cop had him, and consequently was not a bit surprised when the cop offered to forget about any pending criminal charges if he would sign a waiver of prosecution, affirming that at no time did Officer Miller assault or batter him.

Next to Officer Miller was a black guy named Marcus Wells, their passenger. In his late twenties, well-dressed, slim. Buddy had stopped him two weeks earlier for making a left turn at a red light. They found—for real—1.6 pounds of black tar heroin in the trunk.

Turned out Marcus Wells was highly valued by the St. Louis office of the DEA and FBI Task Force. A U.S. attorney spoke to a county district attorney who spoke to the chief and so on. The long and short of it was, the Tulsa PD agreed to transport Marcus Wells to St. Louis and turn him over to the St. Louis office of the DEA. Marcus was just a small cog in a Midwestern drug cartel, and the DEA planned to use him to go after the cartel's unofficial board of directors. So they had been told.

So here they were. One lieutenant and two patrol officers tripping with a mid-level drug courier. The black tar heroin was stored in an evidence kit in the trunk.

They came to a rest stop between Springfield and Rolla, and Van told Buddy to pull in.

Buddy parked the car, while Van looked at his watch. Then Van turned around to Ray and nodded his head.

Van said, "We're going to get out and stretch our legs."

Marcus said, "Lieutenant."

"Maybe smoke a cigarette."

"Lieutenant."

"What is it, Marcus?" Van said. He spoke as if to a child.

"I need to use the restroom."

"Just hold on, Marcus." Van said, "We're going to go first. Get a Coke, and then Ray will take you to the bathroom. Ray, cuff him to the door."

Ray reached over and slipped his key into the handcuffs that were sitting on Marcus's lap. He released the one on Marcus's left hand and hooked it around the armrest and snapped it shut again.

It was an unmarked police car; the back doors didn't open from the inside. A wire cage separated the front and back seats. Van opened the back door for Ray and Ray got out.

"Back in about ten," Van said. "Marcus."

The police officers walked off.

Marcus Wells watched them as they approached the rest room about forty yards away, thinking, cops. No humanity. Arrogant motherfuckers too, acting like they were on some sort of "top secret mission" when they were just transporting him. Hicks.

Marcus owned two cars and lived in an upscale condominium in the Soulard area. He wore a light-colored Armani suit with a black shirt. He dressed well and he spoke well. And he could see that it fucked these hicks all up. Especially the one that rode in the back with him. That one was just aching to take him to a good lynching tree, show him what they did to boys like him in Oklahoma.

The one up front—the lieutenant—he tried to act like he was a high-hat G-man, but he was no better. *Marcus*, Vannerson called him. The man clearly being relieved that Marcus had one of those conveniently niggerish-sounding names. Mar*cus*, Lu*cius*, Lemarrion. Call a man a nigger without saying nigger. Cracker.

Marcus looked forward to arriving in St. Louis so he could show these farm boys how it really was. That they were just a cab service to him, nothing more. He wasn't going to jail. He would turn state's evidence, tell the feds all they wanted to hear. Formally or informally, go into the witness protection program. He hoped they would move him some place that wasn't too cold.

He wondered what he would say to the farm boys when they got there. He had time to think about it. Something to put them in their place, let them know where they stood. Maybe, *thanks for the ride, cowboy. Oh, by the way, did they tell you boys I'm not going to jail? No?* Or, *see you on the back side, redneck.* Or, fuck being clever, just spit in the big cop's face. Or, maybe the little one that had been sitting next to him.

Well, there was time to think about it, think about the best way to play it.

Marcus turned when he heard the door open on the other side of the car. There was another man there. Black guy. Recognition glinted across his face.

"Dave?"

"Marcus," the man said. And pointed a gun with a long-barreled silencer at Marcus and shot him in the face. Then fired two more shots into his chest and body. Marcus slumped over, dead, and the black guy named Dave fired two more bullets into his head.

Dave Mayfield shut the door of the police car and put the gun in his jacket. He walked over to a waiting car and got in. The car drove off.

Two

It was hard to pin it down precisely, but Kessler believed the moment he first got the hots for Judge Carol Macy was when she pointed her finger at him in open court and said, "If you don't stop this right now, I'm going to hold your ass in contempt."

Well . . . hmmmm. Was there something Freudian or masochistic about it? Some deep-seated, personal, pyschosexual thing for authority figures? Or perhaps just something improper, unprofessional . . . somethin' stupid, as Frank and Nancy would croon. Would he stand in line if Carol thought she'd find the time to spend a moment with him?

Paul F. Kessler, attorney-at-law, age thirty-five, moderately respected, stared back at the Honorable Carol Macy, district judge for Tulsa County, trying to comprehend her, himself, this thing called lust. She was about six years older than him, with shoulder-length brown hair of no particular style, a little freckled around the eyes. Brown eyes with a hint of green hazel. Which you could see if you looked close enough. Which Kessler had.

Now he wondered, had she caught him looking? Had she noticed him staring inappropriately during one of the pretrial conferences of *Harris v. Ellis,* thinking that, when you looked beyond the horned-rim glasses and the sexless black robe, when you put aside all the professional considerations that should exist between judge and attorney, the Honorable Carol Jane Macy was really quite a dish.

There was no defending it. It was not the sort of thing you could give voice to. Not to her or anybody. He was a lawyer in a big small town and he didn't care to have the reputation as some anachronistic, sexist asshole who couldn't accept women in professional capacities. Who couldn't just see them as people and leave it at that. He didn't care to have the local legal community think such things about him, even if they were more or less true.

But Carol Macy was a good-looking woman. A womanly woman beneath the judicial exterior, and he couldn't help being attracted to her. She was also a married womanly woman. And a married woman judge at that . . . telling attorney Kessler now, outside the presence of the jury, that if he didn't stop making veiled references to the defendant's insurance coverage, he was going to buy himself a mistrial. And if he did that, if he forced them all to try this three-day case all over again, she would put him in the county jail for a twenty-four-hour period of attitude adjustment.

Kessler said, "Your Honor, I never meant to suggest to the jury that Ms. Ellis was covered by insurance. I only meant—"

"You said 'them,' " the opposing counsel said. "Janet Ellis is sitting at the defense table by herself, see. Where is this 'them'?"

"It's just an expression," Kessler said. "You're reading too much into it."

The insurance company's lawyer, whose name was Mark Warman, said, "You said, 'Don't let them get away with this.' Who is them?"

"It's just an expression. You're being paranoid."

Mark Warman, who was not dumb, said, "Your Honor, Mr. Kessler is trying to suggest to this jury that we've got a big bad insurance company versus the little guy."

Kessler said, "But, you are representing the big bad insurance company, and I am representing the little guy. I'm asking the jury for an award of two hundred fifty thousand dollars. And if I get this jury to award it, State Farm will make out the check. Janet Ellis has a million-dollar umbrella policy. She isn't going to be out anything."

Judge Carol Macy said, "Paul, that's not the point. You know the law in this state. There are not to be any references to insurance coverage in a standard negligence case. Your pretrial motions have prohibited Mr. Warman from suggesting to the jury that Ms. Ellis will personally have to pay for an award, so your client is protected to the degree I can protect him. But don't push me beyond that. Now you can take up the fairness of the statute the next time you write your state legislator, but in this court I'm going to enforce it. And if you try to prevent me from doing that, I will put you in jail." She said, "Do we understand each other?"

Kessler said, "Yes, ma'am."

Yes, ma'am.

The jury awarded Noah Harris two hundred ten thousand dollars to compensate him for his bodily injuries, medical bills, lost wages, pain and suffering, and all other damages. It was less than what Kessler had asked for, but almost twice what State Farm had offered to settle the claim before trial. Mark Warman wasn't especially happy, but he didn't waste a lot of time crying about it either. He came to Kessler ten minutes after the verdict was read and offered to settle the claim again.

Warman said, "I just talked with the claims adjustor. She told me she won't ask me to file an appeal if you agree to take two hundred flat. No interest. The offer is good today."

"Oh bullshit, Mark," Kessler said. "The settlement offer was your idea. Just like the old one was."

Mark Warman held his palm up, showing he was a reasonable man. "I'm playing straight with you, Paul. We appeal and your client won't get anything for a year."

"You appeal, you'll have to put that money up in bond anyway. And when you lose the appeal, you'll owe us another fifteen grand in statutory interest."

"That's if I lose," Mark Warman said. "I don't think I'll lose."

"If you didn't think you'd lose the appeal," Kessler said, "you wouldn't offer anything over thirty. You just want to chip a little away."

Mark said, "No, guy, I'm being completely straight with you," and held on to his serious expression.

Kessler thought, "guy"? But you really had to give the man credit. It was part of what made Mark scary; he could point at a white wall, look you straight in the eye and tell you that that wall was black. Maybe he'd earned something for that.

Besides, you could never be fully sure of what an appellate court would do.

Kessler said, "Make it two-oh-five and we can go home."

Mark Warman smiled and said, "Paul, you are *killing* me."

He'd calculated the fee before he reached his car. Forty percent of two hundred five thousand dollars. A little over eighty thousand. Get three of those a year and you're making a decent living. Not dot-com millionaire money, but money enough. Kessler liked to think he was not overly attached to money. He thought he had most of what he needed. Enough for a decent car, a pleasant three-bedroom house in Zinc Park, a couple of vacations a year. If he ever got the big pop—say, a $200 million products liability verdict against General Motors—he didn't know what he would really change. Buy a few more cars, perhaps. Maybe buy a house north of Paris, bone up on the language and live like Tom Ripley, sans the homicidal tendencies. Tend to the garden and go into the village in the evening for a cappuccino.

And then what? Sit in the café and watch the people go by? Watch "Frasier" reruns with English subtitles? How long before he died of boredom?

Well, it wasn't something to worry about now. Eighty-two thousand was hardly anything to retire on. Still, he felt good about it.

Kessler started the BMW and let it warm for a moment. It was a 1973 3.0 CSI model with light blue paint. A low-slung coupe with slightly Italian-looking lines. It had a five-speed gearshift with a wooden knob. Beautiful, classic, unpretentious. Though not especially practical.

He rolled down the window, using the hand crank. It was late April and the evening was warm. It would cool to around sixty or so when the night came. In a couple of months, the dreaded July and August would come to Oklahoma, driving the people to Grand Lake and cable television. The car would need air-conditioning then. Kessler estimated it would cost at least two thousand to have it installed in the old BMW. It would be worth every penny.

He geared into reverse and glanced at the rearview mirror. No one behind. But, then, he looked again. Something. He adjusted the mirror.

There, in the distance, Carol Macy.

She was wearing a brown skirt and white blouse. She held her jacket in her hand, looking different out of the robes. Standing face to face with a man who looked about ten years her senior. Kessler couldn't hear what she was saying, but she was obviously upset. Putting her face closer to the man's, like she was stressing a point. Kessler saw the man take her arm. Then saw Judge Macy pull her arm away. The man took her arm again, tighter this time, and pulled her closer.

Kessler thought, it's none of your business, it really isn't. But he killed the engine, got out of the car and walked toward them.

As he approached, he made direct eye contact with the man. He was not too big a fellah, Kessler thought. About fifty with thick gray hair, slicked back. Wearing an expensive tan suit. Giving Kessler one of those dead-ass wolf stares. Territorial, he was. He opened his mouth to speak, but Kessler beat him to it.

Kessler said, "How are you doing?"

The man said, "We're doing fine" in a voice that meant: mind your own fucking business. The man said, "Is there something we can help you with?"

"Oh, no," Kessler said. "I thought you might be having car trouble." Kessler held direct eye contact with the man to let him know he knew full well there wasn't any car trouble. Look a man in the eye while you tell the clearest lie and he'll know the truth. And it was in this way that the unspoken, dick-swinging exchange unfolded between them.

What do you want?

I want to make sure you're not about to kick the daylights out of this woman.

What is this, the fifties? She's my wife, you dipshit. Beat it.

I know she's your wife. But I'm going to stay here until things cool down.

Because I grabbed her arm? What makes you think I'm going to inflict any real pain on her?

Just a feeling, buddy. Just a bad feeling.

Kessler stood there and let the silence fill between them.

The man said, "Do you know who I am?"

Kessler said, "No."

"Sam Clay. That's *Chief* Sam Clay, of the Tulsa Police Department. Now I happen to be having a private conversation with my wife."

Kessler nodded, then glanced over at Carol Macy. Her expression said that she understood that Kessler was trying to protect her. It was an expression he'd never seen her wear before. This woman, the Honorable Carol Macy, looking miserable and distressed in the midst of a nasty marital argument. Kessler said, "We've met."

Kessler would later wonder what he had done wrong then. If he had hesitated a little too long in acknowledging knowing Carol or maybe betrayed an attraction by the way he looked at her. He later wondered if his pity for her in this ugly scene had made him more attracted to her and it had come out in his tone. Either there was something in his look or tone that set the man off or the man was just plain nuts. Whatever the reason, Sam Clay's response escalated the situation.

Sam Clay said, "I wouldn't be surprised."

"Fuck you, Sam," Carol Macy said.

"Calm down, honey," Clay said.

"I mean, fuck you," Carol Macy said. "How dare you say that to me. You of all people."

"How dare I what?"

Realizing his plans of smoothing things out were failing and looking to become a full-blown domestic call, Kessler said, "Look, why don't we all go into the police station over there and have a cup of coffee and sort this thing out." Kessler wanted a cop there. Because if he heard this sort of thing going on next door to his house, he would call the police before it got to the point where the man smacks the woman around and the police come along with an ambulance and the woman, holding an icepack to her face, says never mind, never mind.

Clay said, "Son, I just told you. I am the police. Now beat it, before you get yourself involved in something you can't handle."

Carol Macy said, "Paul, just go. It's all right. Go."

Kessler exchanged another look with Sam Clay. The man giving another one of his hard on stares. Kessler saw the gun at the man's side. A black semiautomatic. He realized that Clay caught him looking at it. And in that moment, Clay was telegraphing something to him. Telling him, *yes, that's a gun on my hip and I wouldn't mind using it on you.*

But for some reason, deep down, Kessler was not frightened. That is, his gut told him that Clay wanted him to *believe* he would shoot him, but he, Clay, knew that he would not. Like it was not in his makeup to do it.

Only a gut feeling; not a thing to gamble your life on. Still, Kessler felt much more anger and disgust than fear.

He said to Carol Macy, "Are you sure you'll be okay?" Telling Clay that the decision was hers, not his.

"Really," Carol said. "It's okay."

Kessler turned and walked to his car.

That night, he wondered if he should have called 911 as soon as he got to his car. He went back and forth on it, reminding himself that she was a judge and that they were in the parking lot of the police department, but still wondering if he had been a coward for abandoning her. He remembered seeing a girl at a convenience store crying because her boyfriend had beat her up and now he was looking for her and she was terrified. Kessler and the store cashier and another customer all offered to call the police and spent considerable time trying to persuade her to do it, but she absolutely refused. Awful, but typical. Most of them return home or let him come back.

He told himself to forget about it.

He ran into her two days later.

It's not a hard thing to do in Tulsa—running into people you know, people you work with. A town of roughly half a million people, but all too tightknit. Especially if you were part of the legal community.

Still, Kessler was surprised to see Judge Carol Macy at the coffeehouse. It was a late Saturday afternoon, slow, lazy, only a handful of customers in the place. Kessler was sitting by himself, reading the entertainment section of someone's leftover *Dallas Morning News.*

He lowered the newspaper as Carol Macy walked by. She didn't say hello or acknowledge him in any way. Maybe she'd seen him, maybe she hadn't. He turned to look at her from behind after she had passed. She was at the counter now, placing her order.

She looked good. Wearing one of those short, wraparound skirts with bright colors and a white V-necked T-shirt and sandals. The back of her brown hair somewhat damp, like she had recently taken a shower. Maybe she'd been working in the garden and had cleaned up afterwards. Whatever. She looked damn good.

But, Kessler thought, what did you expect? She's not a nun. She was a figure of authority, older than him, but—what? He had to remind himself that he was thirty-five years old, not a kid anymore. It wasn't a crush, really. An attraction to an attractive woman. Yet he couldn't quite beat back the teasing voice that said, Kessler likes teacher. Yes, he does.

She turned around then, a cup of coffee in one hand and a small white bag in the other. And she busted him, caught him looking right at her. Kessler did his best to get out of it, raising his hand to gesture a hello. And was surprised to hear her say, "What are you doing?" Friendly. Almost flirtatious.

Kessler shrugged. "Just having a lazy day."

She said, "I thought you'd be working."

"It's Saturday."

"I know," the judge said. "But you seem like the diligent type."

"That's just an act," Kessler said.

"I understand you settled the case."

"Yes."

"And the client's happy?"

"Happy enough." The client's attitude was at the peak of the gratitude parabola. This week, Noah Harris thought Paul Kessler was the greatest lawyer a man could have. But after a couple of years passed and the settlement was spent, Noah's perspective might slip down to the other side of the bell curve. He might feel that any lawyer with half a brain could have gotten him two hundred grand, but a good one should have gotten him at least half a million and Paul Kessler had let him down. It was not an uncommon phenomenon. Kessler had experienced it enough that he almost didn't take it personally anymore. The experience had given him a fairly mercenary outlook on the legal profession and, perhaps unfortunately, life itself.

Carol Macy said, "Well, it's good that it's over."

Kessler regarded her then. A beautiful woman in a coffee shop. The sight of her messed up his perspective and he wondered, probably incorrectly, if she had meant something with that remark. He could say, you mean the trial? Then flush as she said, uh, yeah, what did you think I meant, you freak? The beauty of misunderstandings.

"Yeah," he said, "it's good."

Carol remained there for a moment, hesitating before she looked outside.

Kessler said, "Would you like to sit down?"

She hesitated again. Then she scanned the room, seeing if there was anyone there she knew. It was a small town. Kessler realized he'd made her uncomfortable and threw out an exit visa. "If you have time," he said.

Carol Macy gave him a slight smile. It reminded Kessler of the smile she'd given him two days ago. The one that seemed to say, I know what you're up to. She said, "I have time."

He straightened up as she took a seat across the table. He felt awkward, suddenly conscious of himself. He was out of his uniform. Wearing Saturday clothes—khaki pants and a blue

T-shirt, boots. Without the armor of his suit and tie; she without the black robes, sitting there in summer clothes, looking like any other luscious soccer mom. Two people the same as before, only different. Meeting each other for the first time, in a way. Kessler wondered if she felt awkward too. Probably not.

She was sitting at the table with him and he had to tell himself to forget her role, just think of her as her and say the sort of lame shit that regular people say to each other when they have coffee.

"So, what are you up to today?" Kessler said. And immediately felt stupid.

"Oh, nothing much," she said. "I was going to go to the courthouse today and do some work. But maybe I won't. You know how it is after a trial; you're so drained."

"The judge feels that too?"

"No, we just sit up there doing crossword puzzles," she said. "Of course we feel that. We're human too."

"Yeah, I'm noticing that."

She smiled a frown at him. Cheeky monkey.

She said, "Don't try your cornpone charm on me. It won't work."

"Oh, come on. Juries like it."

"Does it actually work with women?"

"Not so much," he said. "I've ruined some good ties, getting drinks thrown on me."

"Drinks? How about hot coffee?"

"Hasn't happened yet."

"It will."

Kessler said, "When I was in college, there was this guy I used to hang out with, he came up with all sorts of approaches. For girls in bars. We were kids then; we didn't know anything. Like that fat guy in *Animal House*, says 'Gee, you think we're gonna score tonight?' "

"Yeah, I remember it." Her tone flat then.

"We were like that. Anyway, this buddy of mine—his name was, uh, Deke Something, he'd go up to a table full of girls and throw a bunch of straws on their table. They'd look up at him and he'd point to the straws and say, 'You got your lions, tigers, and bears' and then move on from there."

Carol Macy said, "I don't get it."

Kessler shrugged. "Neither did they. But that's how he'd get us to the table. Some of them were amused and then we'd start flirting with them."

"That could not have possibly worked."

"Hey, it worked for him. Sometimes, it worked for him. But he had guts."

"You mean, this lions, tigers, and bears . . . he would get girls to sleep with him with that?"

"Sometimes, it worked. Once in a while, he'd get a beer thrown on him. That's what made me think of him—when you talked about throwing drinks on people. We were at a bar and he completely misread this girl. He kept talking to her and she kept telling him to bug off, and then finally he said, 'I'll leave if you can look me in the eye and say, "Deke, you're not the champ." ' And she poured a beer over his head. *Then* said, 'Deke, you're not the champ.' Then she walked out. So he sits there for a couple of moments, not saying anything. Then he asked the bartender for a towel and wiped it off. The whole bar watching him, kind of admiring him. He had style. He got another girl to go home with him."

She smiled. She liked the story. But she said, "What kind of girls were these?"

"It was college. People thought Howie Mandel was funny back then. Deke, he had a sense of what tables to approach, what tables not to approach."

"Would he have approached my table?"

Kessler pondered that for a moment.

He said, "Well, I doubt it."

"Why not?"

"Well, what sort of girl were you back then? I would imagine you were studious and serious."

"I was."

Kessler thought he detected regret in her tone. Wishful thinking perhaps. But she had said she was human too. Around forty and wondering if the path she had set out for herself was the right one. She could tell herself that the kind of girls that had flung with the Dekes of the world had likely flunked out of college and taken jobs at clothing stores, but that didn't mean they hadn't enjoyed themselves. Kessler remembered the valedictorian of his law school class: a girl that seemed ditzy but was almost supernaturally intelligent and had received offers from every top firm in Dallas and Houston but was always complaining about not having a boyfriend. Most of the women law professors couldn't stand her because, to them, her existence was an affront to professional women everywhere. Kessler was not surprised to learn, years later, that she had quit practicing law. She had been difficult to talk to because her neediness was off-putting, but maybe, like a lot of people, she had just been in the wrong place.

Carol said, "And this Deke person, you admired him?"

"Sure," Kessler said. "We all did."

"That's . . . very sad."

"Hey, all guys admire guys like that. They say otherwise, they're lying."

"Right." The woman smiled. "The funny thing is," she said, "it doesn't change when they get older. All men are sixteen-year-old boys."

"Well," Kessler said, "it is what it is." He didn't know what else to say. He wondered if she would want to continue the conversation now, maybe take it into something personal or intimate. Or if she would be wise and say she had to be going. In the background, staff complained about how slow it was. No one comes after two o'clock; why are we open? At a table by the window, a couple of boyish-looking medical students leaned close to each other, whispering for some reason. Outside, the sun was sinking behind what used to be the Cherry Street bakery.

Carol Macy said, "About the other day."

Kessler said, "Yes?"

"I want to thank you for what you did . . ."

"Okay," Kessler said, uncomfortable.

"But . . . it really wasn't necessary."

Kessler took it in.

He said, "I don't understand."

"I'm just saying it wasn't necessary."

A man can be offended sometimes and not quite know why. Not every impulse can be explained, particularly our own. But Kessler was offended now and he was unable to hide it.

He said, "Well forgive me for interfering."

"What are *you* mad about?"

"I'm not mad," Kessler said. "Just say thank you or don't. Don't patronize me."

"No one's patronizing you. I'm just telling you that it wasn't necessary."

The horniest man won't let a beautiful woman push him around. Not if he's got a sizable ego, which Kessler did. And now he was beginning to wonder what her real motives were for joining him.

Kessler said, "You flatter yourself."

Carol Macy said, "Would you mind explaining that." Her voice hard now, using that authoritative judge tone. Her courtroom voice.

But they weren't in a courtroom now. If she wanted to have his ass thrown in jail, she'd have to call a cop.

He said, "You tell me my stepping in wasn't necessary. Why? I'll tell you. It's because you're afraid I'll think you're common or something. White trash, like the rest of us. Well, you needn't worry, ma'am. I'm not going to tell anyone what I saw that day. In fact, I haven't even given it much thought. It's your business. Your life. So don't waste your time trying to justify it to me. *That* isn't necessary."

Boy, did that seem to make her mad. Had she not been a public official, he'd've thought she'd tell him to fuck off. She didn't though. She just stared at him for a few moments.

She said, "God, they're right. You are an asshole."

"Yeah," Kessler said. "But I'm not a creep."

There was an awful, uncomfortable silence after that where they both looked away from each other. Hard feelings and confusion and not a little curiosity. But it passed after a while, and what happened next was kind of strange.

Instead of leaving, Carol Macy looked straight at him for a long time, neither frowning nor smiling.

"No," she said quietly. "You're not a creep."

Kessler shifted in his chair, starting to feel a little bit shitty.

"Listen," he said. "Maybe this wasn't such a good idea."

"No," she said. "It's all right."

"I only meant—"

"It's all right."

Then they looked at each other, direct eye contact, there, and something seemed to change between them. In modern terms, a paradigm shift or moment of clarity. Something. In any event, Carol Macy said, "What are you doing tonight?"

Kessler said, "What?"

"What are you doing tonight?"

Kessler thought, do I call her Your Honor? Or Carol? He

said, "I don't have any plans. Would you"—what?—"like to have dinner or something?"

"No," Carol Macy said. "No dinner. We can't be seen in a public place. I'm a public official."

Married to another public official, Kessler thought. Still, he heard himself say, "There's a bar at Ninety-first and Sheridan. A dump, really. Tommie's. No one—that we would know—would be there. We could meet there."

Carol Macy said, "Ten o'clock?"

"Okay."

She stood up and slung her bag strap over her shoulder. Very businesslike about it. But then said, "Paul?"

"Yes?"

"You can call me Carol, you know."

Kessler said, "Well, now what would be the fun in that?"

She pointed her index finger at him. Just as she had done in court when she threatened to have him jailed. "Careful," she said. Then walked out.

He watched her as she pushed herself out the door, then walked in front of the plate-glass window. Then reaching the corner, turning, gone.

It was then that he wondered: did that actually happen? If he were to repeat it to Hank Patterson or another close friend, would they believe it? If the tree falls in the forest and no one's there to videotape it, did it actually fall? Well, too soon to form any conclusions yet. Tonight would tell what tonight would tell. She was married. To a cop. To the chief of police, actually. As love affairs go, it certainly wouldn't qualify as simple and carefree. But, by God, it was exciting, and she was sexy beyond words.

Years later, he would think back to this moment and wish that some sort of guardian angel had stepped in then and told him to pull his head out of his ass. It would have saved him a lot of trouble. . . . But then he knew he probably wouldn't have listened. Not after she pointed the you're-a-naughty-boy finger at him like that. He wouldn't have listened to anybody.

THREE

A low-level strip mall. Dark. A handful of cars and pickup trucks in the parking lot. Sewing supplies store, Chinese food, a used bookstore with a sign that read, "Used Bookstore." And Tommie's tucked into the corner.

It wasn't much better inside. Two levels, the higher one darker than the lower, lit only by the glow of a wide-screen television. Lighter on the lower level, two large box lamps hanging over two pool tables. Ugly and depressing, but harmless enough. A suburban dive.

Kessler took a seat at the bar and ordered a Bushmills. There were maybe five other people in the place. College kids home for the summer, catching up on how little they knew each other. There was a baseball game on the big-screen television. "Cheers" was on the small television behind the bar. Kessler watched "Cheers."

When he saw Carol come in, it became real again. She was still wearing that same wraparound skirt, God bless her, but had a blue pullover sweater over the white T-shirt. She looked even more beautiful now, more natural and approachable. Soccer Mom Galore.

She smiled at him as she came up. "Hi," she said. Kessler said the same thing back and before he could get anything else out, she said, "Let's get a table." Wrapping up the prelims quickly as women do.

Kessler said, "Okay."

She pointed to what was probably the darkest corner of the bar. "That one," she said.

Kessler said, "Okay."

As she was walking away, she said, "And get me a vodka tonic. Absolut."

"Yes, ma'am."

Kessler gave the bartender an I-just-do-what-I'm-told expression that hopefully left him with some dignity, then ordered her drink. When he walked it over to her, he noticed the cigarette in her hand.

"You smoke?" he said.

Carol Macy exhaled. "On occasion," she said. "Disappointed?"

"No."

"Surprised?"

"Yeah, a little."

"Do you smoke?"

"Only when I'm nervous."

"Are you nervous now?"

"Sure."

"No, you're not."

They sipped their drinks.

Carol said, "What are you looking at?"

Kessler said, "The way you're dressed. It's not what I expected."

"It's how I was dressed earlier today."

"I know, but—"

"Did you think I'd come here in a trenchcoat or something? Like a spy movie?"

Kessler said, "Well, I thought. I don't know."

"Maybe you *are* nervous," Carol said. "Are you Catholic?"

"What?"

"Catholic."

"No."

"Used to be?"

"Sort of," Kessler said. "My mother was Irish Catholic. My father, he's, well, he's not very religious."

"Your mother died?"

He said, "About a year ago."

"I'm sorry," she said.

"It's all right. Part of life, I suppose."

"Is your father German?"

"Yes." Kessler said, "Good Alva stock." Which was nonsense, if you knew Jim Kessler. But he wouldn't tell her that.

"You're from Alva? I grew up in Enid."

"Is that right?" Kessler said. "I always thought you were from here."

"No. Enid born and bred."

"Macy's not German."

"No . . . Hoehner," Carol said. "That's my mother's name. She was something. And her parents . . . oh my God. Her mother barely spoke English. My grandfather, he died when I was about three. My grandmother lived with us. She was a character. She used to say that I-35 cut the state of Oklahoma into two perfect halves. West of it was good German, Dutch stock, working the land and building things. East of it, she said, was just trash."

"And now you live east of it."

"Yes," Carol said, "Part of the occupying presence."

"Enid," Kessler said. "Are you kin to Glenn Macy?"

"Yes. He's my younger brother. Did you know him?"

"Yeah, I wrestled him."

"Excuse me?"

"In high school," Kessler said. "He wrestled for Chisum and I wrestled for Alva High. He was a good wrestler."

"Who won?"

"I did."

"You were good?"

"I was," Kessler said. "I was thinner then."

"Glenn used to do things to keep his weight down. Eat potatoes raw, like they were apples. One time he kept spitting in a cup, just to get rid of saliva. My mother saw it and almost threw up."

"Yeah, it's a sickness."

"So you miss that?" she said. "Rolling on the ground with men?"

"Not really. Do you?"

"Oh, shut up," she said. "Get me another drink."

He got her another drink.

When he returned, she said, "I understand you were in the Army."

Kessler said, "Yeah, JAG Corps."

"Get to go overseas?"

"Yeah. Most of my tour was in West Germany."

"How was that?"

"It was nice. I liked Europe."

"Do you miss it?"

"Only during July and August. They don't get the sort of heat we do. Apart from that, no, not especially. Being from a small town, I took a pride in adapting to Europe. The coffee, the beer, the pace, the way they put careers in the right perspective . . . there was a lot I liked about it. But I got homesick for the States. I got homesick for this place."

"Tulsa?"

Kessler shrugged. "Yeah. It's overcast there most of the time. You don't think it will affect your mood, but it does. Eight, ten days of it in a row will get you down. Maybe it explains their outlook on life. I don't know. You know where Europeans like to go when they come here? Not New York. They take vacations in Texas."

"Really?"

"Yes. The English especially. They love Texas. Something about the wide open spaces, being able to go to a Super Wal-Mart, and all the sunshine. They even like the heat. They go there in August. The Germans, they're nuts about the West. Rocky Mountains, Grand Canyon. They love Indian stuff."

"India—"

"No, Indians. American Indians. I'd tell them where I was from and they'd ask me what a reservation was like. And then there would be the lecture about the Trail of Tears and how we elected the butcher of the Creek Nation president."

"Who was that?"

"Andrew Jackson."

"Hmmm."

"Yeah, you get a lotta lectures on human rights in Germany."

It took a moment for Carol Macy to smile.

"You're a cynic," she said.

"Oh, not really. I didn't hate anyone, even the people giving me shit. One on one, the French are very nice. If you try to speak French and don't wear, you know, Dallas Cowboys sweat-shirts. And the English are some of the nicest people you can drink with. But . . . well, maybe I am a little cynical. I mean, there are all sorts of injustices, little people getting fucked over now, today, right here in front of us, and most people don't give a shit about it. This focus on the sins of history, there's a certain arrogance there. A laziness. The point is not to help, but to show you that you're morally superior. But we got plenty of that here too." Kessler became conscious of what he was saying. Preaching. "Sorry," he said.

"No, it's all right."

Kessler said, "What did you do before being put on the bench?"

"In-house counsel at Williams Companies."

Kessler reflected on that. In-house counsel at Williams to Tulsa County District Court—a likely cut in pay. He said, "Do you miss that?"

Carol said, "No. I was dying of boredom."

Kessler said, "Do you have mixed feelings about being in the political arena?"

She looked at him briefly, debating whether or not he had pushed too far. She said, "Do you mean, do I miss having a private life?"

"Yeah, that's partly what I mean."

"Isn't that obvious?"

"No, it isn't that obvious. You're rather guarded."

"And you're rather nosy."

"Well, I figure we gotta talk about something."

Carol smiled. "I think I may have been wrong about you. You're not really an asshole. You are a smartass, though. And somewhat naïve too."

"Wait a minute, earlier you said I was a cynic."

"That too."

"Well, what *do* you mean?"

"Do you want me to tell you the whole story of my crappy marriage? When it started to go bad. What happened to Us. How we don't talk anymore. That we haven't made love in six months. And so on." She said, "Listen, I'm not a kid. We don't have to . . . justify this. Okay?"

Kessler put his hand on her thigh. Started to caress it.

"Okay," he said.

Carol Macy said, "Good."

She leaned over and kissed him. One, two . . . three and her mouth opened up and she was flicking her tongue in and out of his mouth, opening up now, letting out years of a woman's passion, a need. Her arms went around his neck and pulled him toward her tight and Kessler could feel the strength in her grip, enough that it almost made him laugh. Jesus, woman . . .

Kessler said, "Let's get out of here."

They walked out to his car and got in. Kessler started it and she said, "Where do you live?"

"In Zinc Park."

About a fifteen-minute drive from there.

Carol pointed her finger toward the back of the building.

"In the alley," she said.

Kessler drove the car into the alley and pulled it up to a stop. He turned off the engine and looked over to her. She was reclining the seat back as far as it would go. She pulled her underpants off and hiked her skirt up. Then she reached for him, pulled him over and held him above her, undid his belt and slid down his trousers. She pulled him down, then guided him inside her and then began rocking her hips.

Kessler said, "You're marvelous."

She mentally rolled her eyes. She wanted to tell him to shut up and just *fuck her*, fuck her now. But she had never said that to any man, had never talked like that because it was not appropriate for a woman to talk like that, it was animal to talk like that, to think like that, but she felt animal now, animal and alive.

Carol Macy said, "Shush." And then she was moaning. Because she could feel it now, she was getting there. The first orgasm she had had in years. It was happening, happening, and then she was coming, coming in waves as she cried out and Kessler was shushing her now because he didn't want to be discovered by a night watchman, have a flashlight beam shined into the car while this woman's legs were wrapped around him, and then they came together, shuddering and murmuring and then panting with excitement and exhaustion and emotion.

Ten, maybe twelve seconds of silence.

Carol Macy said, "Do you think we can do it again?"

Kessler said, "Not here."

FOUR

The ref blew his whistle and T. J. Vannerson immediately went to the cowboy's stance: knees bent, feet apart, hands held up like a dancing bear. He circled and weaved, and then quickly lashed out and grabbed his opponent's wrist. His opponent, a red-haired boy from Edmond North, yanked back, but T.J. held on to four fingers and squeezed. The red-haired boy winced in pain, and T.J. charged in, hard. Using his other arm, he captured a leg, put all his weight on it and shoved. The red-haired boy went down.

Van yelled, "All right, T.J.! All right! Get him on his back . . . keep moving! Get him!"

T.J. kept moving, but not like he planned. The red-haired boy kept cool and rolled, pulling T.J. over on his back. Like the whole thing had been his idea. The crowd from Edmond roared in approval, while the parents of Edison High groaned.

Lola Vannerson placed a hand on her husband's back to comfort him, and Van shook his head in disgust. He yelled, "Get him, T.J.!" again. He didn't know what else to say. He'd played football when he was in high school. He hadn't wrestled and he did not understand the principles of the sport. Didn't understand one of the chief rules: always be the bullfighter, not the bull.

The red-haired boy pulled T.J. out of the fire by attempting an illegal full-nelson hold. The ref blew the whistle and separated them. T.J. improved after that, mainly because he began to adhere to the shouted counsel of his coach rather than his father. He didn't manage to pin the red-haired boy, but he won by points. Barely.

Still, after the match, Van grabbed T.J.'s arm affectionately, rubbed his hair, and said, "That's what I'm talking about. That's how you take him down." And Lola stroked her son's back and told him how wonderful he was.

Van said, "You need to work on those takedowns, though. Start pinning these boys."

"Van," Lola said.

"I'm just saying."

"Van, hush. He won, okay?"

T.J. said, "Coach said if I can get down to one fifteen, I can start at the regionals next month."

"Oh, no," Lola said. "He wants you to cut more weight? You're skin and bone as it is."

"Baby," Van said. "It's competition. He can start eating again when school's out."

"Van, don't encourage him." Lola Vannerson said, "Well, let's talk about it tomorrow. T.J., you want to go to Braum's for a banana split?"

"Mom, I'm kinda old for that," T.J. said. He would start driving next year. But he saw his father looking at him then, the expression telling him he should humor his mother. "Well, okay."

Lola and T.J. rode in the Ford Expedition while Van followed in his silver take-home Crown Vic. They met with other parents and kids at Braum's and watched the Edison High mat-maids circle around T.J. like he was Justin Timberlake. Blonde-haired, beautiful boy drawing the girls like flies. Van studied the girls. Fifteen, sixteen, seventeen . . . man, not looking much different than some of the girls at Cassy's.

Van said, "We'll be grandparents before long."

Lola said, "Van, stop it. They're just flirting."

He smiled at his wife. She was a beautiful woman. Blonde, long-legged girl he'd met when he was in college. They'd been married for eighteen years. She worshipped him and the boy. They had two other children, girls. But T.J. was Lola's star. She hardly tried to hide her preference for him.

Van said, "I'm going to have to drop by the station. I'll be home later."

Lola said, "Do you want me to wait up?"

"No. I might be late."

He drove to the parking garage of the Promenade mall, across the road from the new movie theater. He found a spot close to the entrance and parked. He shut off the engine and waited.

About a half-hour later, a dark Lexus LS400 pulled in and drove past him.

Van saw the rental tag on the back and thought, that's him. He watched as the car continued down the length of the garage and turned up the ramp to the second floor. He got out of his car and walked to the stairs. When he got to the next floor, he saw that the Lexus was there. He stepped back between two cars and crouched.

The driver of the Lexus walked by and went toward the elevator. Van fell quickly in behind him.

The elevator doors stopped on Van's arm and then reopened. Van stepped in.

The man inside the elevator was startled by it and made a move toward his jacket pocket, shit, reaching for a gun.

"Easy," Van said. Though he was ready to draw himself.

The man looked at him briefly, tensely, and then relaxed. He said, "You were supposed to meet me inside."

Van said, "I know."

Dave Mayfield smiled. "You don't trust me," he said.

"I wanted to make sure you were alone."

"I didn't know you cared." Mayfield said, "How do I know you didn't bring a backup?"

"You don't."

"My, my, my," Mayfield said. "All this distrustfulness. You cops are more paranoid than the crooks. I thought we were friends."

The elevator door opened. They stepped out, and began walking.

Mayfield said, "They investigating you?"

Van said, "Of course not. Not criminally. They're doing an administrative investigation, see if I should get a slap on the wrist for negligence. That's the general extent of it." He looked at Mayfield. "Don't worry about me," he said.

"I do worry," Mayfield said.

Van ignored that.

But Mayfield said, "Bad police officer, walking off and leaving the dirty drug dealer all by his lonesome. How irresponsible. Well, maybe you can donate some of your money to the policemen's ball."

Van could have told him that they quit having policemen's balls about fifteen years ago. But he didn't want to get too familiar with Mayfield. The guy was a fucking turd drug dealer, after all. And he didn't like Mayfield reminding him about the money. There were parameters to this relationship, boundaries to be respected.

Van said, "He had it coming."

Mayfield turned to look at the cop. "How do you figure?"

"What?"

"Why do you say Marcus had it coming?" Mayfield said. "Did you even know him?"

"No, I didn't know him."

"Then why do you say that?"

Van sighed, show the man he was getting tired. He said, "Why do I say what?"

Mayfield stopped and turned to him. They stood in the shadow of a Chevy Suburban. Mayfield said, "Is it because he was a drug dealer?"

"Are you angry at me or something?" Van said. "You're the one that killed him."

Mayfield shook his head.

"That was business, Van. It had to be done. Marcus had turned snitch. He was about to go to the DEA and make my people very unhappy. It had to be done. Doesn't mean I took any pleasure in it."

"Was he your friend?"

"My friend?" Mayfield said. "Man, you missing my point. No, he wasn't my friend. He was one of these boys you see on the college campuses, puts on some nice clothes and a pair of glasses and says things like 'conducive to' like he's a Ph.D. or something, but he's still just a jackboy. No, I can't say I enjoyed his company." Mayfield said, "But he wasn't evil, you see? He wasn't my friend, but he wasn't a piece of shit either. He was a snitch, that's all. Do you see what I'm talking about?"

Van's expression was bored. "No, I don't."

"The point is, officer, I don't judge him. I don't tell myself that he deserved to die. I just do it. You see?"

"Yeah, whatever," Van said, suppressing a sudden desire to tell this spook to shut the fuck up. He wasn't making much sense. And he was starting to cross the line with this officer shit. "Listen," Van said, "you got what you wanted. I delivered him as promised. I held up my end of the agreement. You gonna hold up yours?"

Mayfield studied Van with a mixture of curiosity and contempt.

He said, "I have the money."

Van regarded Mayfield in return. Mayfield owed him another fifty thousand. That was the deal: fifty before and fifty after. A tax-free hundred grand for about one day's work. Looking at the man now, Van contemplated trading the second fifty for the opportunity of beating him into submission, teach him some respect. If not for him, then for the badge. *I have the money,* he says. Like he hadn't made up his mind yet to give it over. What next: *you want to try and take it from me, muthafucka?* For what? Because he hadn't shown the proper respect for a spook that *he'd* offed? Try making sense of these people. Well, fuck him. Let him do his tough nigger act. He wasn't going to be baited into losing his cool. Mayfield would either hand it over or get a Glock screwed in his ear.

Van said, "Why don't we get it taken care of then. It's late."

Mayfield dragged it out for another minute, and then relaxed again, deciding to put it away for now. He pulled his sweater up. Underneath was a money belt. He undid it and handed it to Van.

"It's all in there," he said. "You can count it if you like, but I'd rather you didn't do it out here."

"Don't worry," Van said. "If I have any complaints, I know how to reach you."

FIVE

It was hard to comprehend, the sight of her on his bed. Call it good fortune or just plain fortune, but it was hard to comprehend the sight of Carol Macy sitting cross-legged on his bed wearing his plaid green bathrobe, smoking a cigarette. "I'm shy," she said. Which didn't make a lot of sense, given the abandon with which she'd wrapped her legs around him in an alley. Then straddled him like a motorcycle in his bed. But then he'd known too many women to understand them. Now, the sight of her afterwards, wearing his bathrobe, with the lamp on, fully exposed, was somehow more difficult to believe than her thrashing around naked in the dark. For it was in the light that you could see that it was the same woman who had threatened to have him jailed for contempt just days ago. It couldn't be her, yet it was. Now she looked at him.

"I'm sorry," she said.

"For what?"

"For calling you an asshole."

"When did you do that?"

"In the coffee shop. Remember, 'They're right; you are an asshole.' "

"Oh, that. That didn't bother me." It didn't, either. "I've been called all sorts of names."

She smiled. "John Stearns really does not like you."

"Judge Stearns? What'd I do to him?"

"Something about a Motion to Reconsider."

Now Kessler smiled. "Yeah," he said. "I remember that."

Judge John Stearns, former associate general counsel of some state agency that regulated dentistry, had granted summary judgment to the City of Bristow on a First Amendment civil rights claim. Kessler represented the plaintiff, who had sued the City of Bristow. The judge issued a written order holding that the plaintiff could not assert a federal claim because it had already been previously litigated in arbitration. Ergo, plaintiff was "collaterally estopped" from proceeding with a federal suit and his case was dismissed.

It turned out to be something of a procedural mess, and it was partly Kessler's fault. The collateral estoppel defense was one of approximately fourteen raised by the city in its motion for summary judgment. It was a lame argument, and you could tell the city attorney's heart wasn't much in it. Consequently, Kessler didn't take it as seriously as he should have and failed to refer to the controlling U.S. Supreme Court case—*McDonald v. City of West Branch*—that specifically holds First Amendment claims cannot be preempted with an arbitration hearing held pursuant to a collective bargaining agreement. It was, as Al Gore would say, the controlling legal authority. A slam dunk, as far as the legal question went.

But Kessler had neglected to consider Judge Stearns himself. Had he done so, maybe he would have learned that John Stearns was one of those results-oriented judges who cared less for the law than forging his own public policy. Had Kessler known that, he'd have been more careful and written a stronger brief. The courts are full of such bench legislators, political appointees who feel the blood of Solomon coursing through their veins. On both sides of the political spectrum.

Judge Stearns had his own agenda. He believed that First Amendment claims were something lazy public employees exploited and made up just to cause trouble at the workplace.

He didn't think much of employment claims in general and hated plaintiffs' lawyers in particular, though no one could ever really tell why. In any event, he was obviously searching for a reason to dismiss the plaintiff's claim against the City of Bristow, and he believed he'd found one in this thing called collateral estoppel.

After he'd written the order dismissing the case, Kessler filed a Motion to Reconsider attaching the *McDonald* case, wherein the Supreme Court specifically ruled that courts couldn't do what Judge Stearns had done. The city's reply conceded that *McDonald* was applicable, but argued that there were many other reasons to dismiss the case, none of which were very convincing. Judge Stearns was stuck. If he didn't reverse himself, he knew he'd be reversed by the Court of Appeals. If he issued another order giving different reasons for dismissing the case, he'd expose his own intellectual dishonesty, and, consequently, would again be reversed by the Court of Appeals. And if he reversed himself, he feared he would look like a fool. Which is, of course, the ultimate terror for the chickenshit public official.

Stearns tried to resolve this dilemma by using the tactic common to the unimaginative: raw bullying. He called Kessler into his chambers and bawled him out, saying this was all his fault for not bringing the *McDonald* case to the court's attention, the case was just a mess and so forth. He said, really, the best way to handle this was just to dismiss it and refile it.

Of course, this made no sense whatsoever. But it would have taken the case off Judge Stearns's hands and spared him what he chose to consider an embarrassment. Kessler said he really couldn't do that, and Stearns said he *strongly* recommended that Kessler consider it, and Kessler finally said, "You can dismiss it, Judge, but I'm not going to."

Judge Stearns actually said, "Well, goddamn!"

It got worse from there. Because Stearns had yelled at Kessler in front of the city attorney, the city attorney got the idea that Stearns wouldn't treat Kessler very well at trial. And he was right about that. On the first day of trial, every one of the city attorney's objections was sustained. And every one of Kessler's was overruled. And Judge Stearns made a point of looking bored or rolling his eyes when Kessler's witnesses testified. Once, while he was cross-examining the city manager, Judge Stearns said, "Just get on with it, Mr. Kessler."

And so it went. But halfway through the trial, Kessler could see that the jury was beginning to resent Stearns too. Americans like a fair fight, and Stearns's prejudice was too obvious. Kessler picked up on the jury's sentiment and used it. Subtly at first, and then not so subtly. Finally, Judge Stearns sustained an objection that was plainly egregious, the unfairness of it clear to everyone in the courtroom, and Kessler seized the moment, saying with all the indignation he could muster against the city attorney and Judge Stearns, "Gentlemen, there will be justice in this trial."

The tactic had been suggested in a Vincent Bugliosi book, and Kessler didn't hesitate to use it. The master himself would have been impressed. The comment got Kessler a thorough chewing-out and a $500 fine, but it was worth it. The jury awarded his client $110,000 in damages. Judge Stearns had to award attorney fees on top of that, as it was a section 1983 case, around $195,000 in all.

Now it pleased him to hear that Stearns still bore a grudge. Because it proved he'd been right about him all along; he really was a small man.

Carol Macy, sitting in a way almost to expose herself, said, "He said you were arrogant."

"A man like that really shouldn't be a judge," Kessler said.

"Oh, come on. You really believe that?"

"I do." Kessler said, "You're not friends with him, are you?"

Carol shrugged. "He is one of the tribe," she said. "Actually, he's a good guy."

Kessler looked at her skeptically. For a moment he was reminded of his college days, when fraternity brothers used the term "good guy" to describe the most degenerated psychopaths on campus so long as they wore a Phi Kappa Kap T-shirt. It didn't make much sense then either.

Still . . . there she was, Mrs. Ma-a-cy. Sitting cross-legged on his bed, one very deliciously soft-looking thigh extending out of the folded bathrobe. Under these circumstances, who was he to judge? He slid his hand up her leg.

He said, "What do you call this tribe?"

"The League of Justice."

His hand was on the sash around her waist, tugging it lightly.

"At these meetings, do you wear anything under the robe?"

"No, it's pretty much like this."

"You're a very naughty girl."

Six

The bouncer kept a taut hold of the young man's hair all the way out the front door. The bouncer knew his trade: usually there was no need for fisticuffs; where the hair goes, the head goes, and where the head goes, the body will follow.

The young man with long blonde hair had made a grab for one of the girls. He was warned twice to keep his hands to himself. He didn't listen. He heard the dancer call out "Merle!", but was still surprised when he felt his hair almost being pulled out of his head. Goddamn slacker.

On the way out, they went by the main stage. Tarra and Sandy were up there, dancing topless, grinding dutifully up against the fire station poles. A couple of the customers whooped in appreciation, but most of them kept stone-silent in the dark. Typical.

Monty Bates sat with Greg Vannerson at a table near the rear. Neither one of them paid attention to the screaming young man. Monty had his bourbon. Van sipped from a cup of coffee.

Monty said, "All right, who do you want there?"

"Same as last time: Sherry, Rose—" Van nodded toward the stage. "Tarra too. And the rest. It's going to be at the Ramada Inn in Okmulgee."

Monty said, "Friday night? You're gonna take my girls away on a Friday night? That's a couple a thousand dollars of business there."

Van shrugged. "What do you want from me?" he said. "I tell

you that's the only time we can do it, that's the only time we can do it. I can't change the guy's birthday."

"Yeah, but Friday night, Van."

"Monty, you know how it is. Come on. We've been doing this for five years. You think I'd take advantage of you?"

"I don't know."

"Monty. Come on." Van said, "You know how it is. My interests are your interests."

The name of the "gentlemen's club" was Cassiopia's, Cassy's for the regulars. Monty Bates was the owner. He was around forty, a thin, dark-haired man with a thin mustache, contrasting with the thick set of handlebars on Van's lip. He wore Calvin Klein jeans, tight to the waist, and a starched orange shirt. There was a Southern air to him, more Alabama than Okie. A hint of drunken, fallen gentility. Some of the cops thought he might be a fag, but that was his business. It was the early evening, and Monty was on his seventh bourbon.

When people asked what Lt. Greg Vannerson would be doing in his club, Monty told them Van was his security advisor. And he was, in a way.

Running a club where women danced half-naked on a stage in front of men was perfectly legal. Running a house of prostitution was not. Cassy's was both a gentlemen's club and a brothel. Monty had been arrested seven years earlier for these activities. He hired a smart lawyer and managed to cut a plea and avoid jail. But it cost him a lot of money. And while he had put on a macho "it's the cost of success" front for those who knew him, the prospect of a prison sentence had scared the shit out of him.

It spooked him more when Lt. Greg Vannerson started coming to his club a few months after he cut the plea. But Van pulled him aside one day, offered to buy him a drink, and started telling him his philosophy. Van started off by asking him, what really was the difference between a lap dance and an old-fashioned lay?

Monty had said, "About three hundred dollars."

Van had laughed. But Monty was wary.

It took a few meetings, but Van eventually convinced Monty he wasn't trying to set him up. The clincher was when Van brought in half a dozen off-duty police officers and let them take the girls to the back room for Las Vegas–type recreation. Then Van had them chip in $150 apiece for a hosting fee.

Later Van said to Monty, see? Van said, now, you've got police officers who are customers. We're all in it together now.

That's how Monty and Van became partners.

They had been doing it now for five years. Cassy's had never been investigated by the police. Some people suspected Chief Clay himself knew what was going on and had no intention of doing anything to stop it. Van, on the other hand, didn't suspect that at all. He knew Sam Clay knew all about Cassy's.

Now Monty smiled and said, "Van, you're blowing smoke up my ass like a politician. Equal partners, bullshit. There ain't a doubt in my mind you're getting more out of this arrangement than I'll ever know." Monty, something of a politician himself, quickly added, "Not that I mind, Van."

There was a girl standing at their table.

Van said, "What's up, Jamie?"

Jamie Flatt was not one of the Cassy dancers. Nor was she a prostitute. She was a waitress. At thirty-one, she was older than most of the dancers. She had long thick hair that was dyed a reddish brown shade and a nice firm figure. She wore tight white pants and a T-shirt that exposed her midriff.

Jamie said, "I need to talk to you."

"Sit down," Van said.

She glanced uncomfortably at Monty. Van gestured with his head and Monty got up and left. Jamie sat down.

Van said, "What is it?"

Jamie said, "You're not gonna believe this."

"Just tell me, Jamie."

"It's about Sam."

"Sam Clay?"

"Yes."

Van leaned back and sighed.

He said, "I told you."

"I know you told me. I only went with him a couple of times. He took me to a nice place; a steakhouse in Sapulpa. It was nice at first. Nice to be taken to dinner, away from this place. You know how it is."

"I know," Van said. "But I warned you not to get involved with him. There are girls here for Sam. Leave them to him."

"He wants me to be his mistress."

Van shrugged. "Is that so bad?"

Jamie frowned, disgusted.

Van said, "I'm not saying he'd be paying you for it or anything. Just . . . would it be so bad to be the man's girlfriend?"

"Yeah, it would," Jamie said. "I mean, look at him, Van. Look at him."

Van looked at her, uncomprehending.

"You don't understand, do you." She said, "The man knows nothing about women. Nothing. He doesn't know what to say; he doesn't know what to do. He's one of these guys who probably didn't get laid until his first marriage, got successful, powerful, in his career, and then decides at the age of fifty that he needs to be some sort of ladies' man. When he tries to be sexy . . . Van, it's embarrassing. It's creepy too."

"I told you."

"I know you told me," Jamie said. "Look, I didn't fuck him or nothing. I just went out with him twice and that was that."

"Sure?"

"All right, he tried to take me to a hotel the last time, and I said, 'Sam, no.' And he got pissed. Said 'What the fuck is your problem?' It scared me, but not so much. He yelled some more, but drove me home."

"Sounds like it's resolved, then."

"No, it's not fucking resolved, Van." Jamie said, "It is not resolved. Last night, he waited for me. He accosted me."

"What do you mean?"

"He waited for me. Here. In the parking lot. He waited until I got off work and walked out to my car. He walked right up to me. Oh, Van, it was gross. He asked me why I hadn't called him, where had I been, told me I shouldn't be avoiding him. *Told* me. And he was touching me. He was touching my arm, my leg. Then he touched me here."

She pointed to her exposed tummy.

She said, "And he said, 'You call me now.' Like it was an order. Van, it scared me."

"All right, all right. Don't get upset now. Don't cry. We'll get it taken care of." He reached out and patted her hand. "I'll look into it."

"I'm not crying," she said. "Listen, do you want some coffee or . . ."

"No. Just take a break." He said, "I'll take care of it, Jamie."

She left him alone to think on it, and he did.

In part, Van felt responsible for the situation. He had brought Sam to the club and set him up with a couple of the working girls. And if he hadn't done that, Sam would have never laid eyes on Jamie. He was supposed to stick with the merchandise, the fucking idiot. With the working girls. And he had at first. Van had selfish reasons for bringing Sam here. Though Sam hadn't paid the girls directly, Van had him nailed all the same. After doing the nasty with Tarra and Rose, Chief Clay would be in no position to come after Van for his role in the operation. Or for anything else. Looking back, the setup had been so easy. The chief had come to one of the officers' birthday parties, drank too much and before he knew it he was on his back in a backroom being straddled by a prostitute.

Van had read that this sort of thing had been practiced for at least since the time of Caesars. By lobbyists, politicians, and businessmen. Give a man a whore and you've got him. He's gratefully extorted. Especially a high-profile cop. There were public men who weren't so dumb. Men like the Reverend Billy Graham. Van had read about him too, in *Parade Magazine*. The Reverend Graham said he made it a policy never to be left alone in a room with any woman not his wife. He didn't explain why. But Van was pretty sure he understood. Old Billy knew his weaknesses and this was one temptation that he was going to avoid. Smart man, Billy Graham. Smarter than Sam Clay.

Van had taken the extra step of videotaping Sam's romp with Tarra. It was a seedy, distasteful thing to do, but it was necessary. He hadn't told Sam he'd done that. But Van suspected that, deep down, Sam knew he had. It explained Sam letting him alone to conduct police work as he saw fit. At the Tulsa Police Department, nobody had more autonomy than Lieutenant Greg Vannerson.

Which is really all Van wanted. He did not want to hurt Sam Clay; he just wanted the insurance. The protection. Personally, he had nothing against Sam. As Van saw it, Sam was just a man trying to get through life as best he could, like anyone else. Like any man, he was entitled to his recreation.

But, goddammit, why did he have to chase after Jamie? She wasn't a whore. She was just a girl. Pretty cool one, too. She'd had a tough life. Shitty upbringing, abusive father. Shitty marriage to some turd who ran off to Montana, leaving her with a kid. She was a cocktail waitress, that's all, working to put food on the table for her and her kid. She didn't deserve this.

Van had never had any sort of sexual relationship with Jamie Flatt. Nor had he ever really wanted to. But he was fond of Jamie and he considered her a friend. And he liked that she had come to him with her problem. She was a good lady. She deserved better. She didn't deserve to be harassed or bullied by anyone. Not even the chief.

The chief. Shit. It would have to be handled carefully. With a certain amount of tact. He would have to back the chief off without bruising the man's ego. Lean on him gently without threatening him. Somehow, it would have to be done. Jamie had come to him, put her faith in him. He would not let her down.

SEVEN

Attorney Bill Wilkinson stood behind the podium and took off his jacket, revealing a starched shirt as white as his hair. He raised his voice and said, "In this corner weighing approximately two hundred pounds, with fourteen hundred wins and no losses, the reigning champion of employment law: Pat Cremin!" A few people laughed.

It was a labor law seminar.

Lawyers are required to get twelve hours of continuing legal education (CLE) a year. School. It meant sitting through ordeals like this at the Tulsa County Bar Association (TCBA) and listening to people like Pat Cremin, Bill Wilkinson, and Jim Priest trying to monologue their way through the material like Jay Leno. The subjects had titles like "Employment at Will after *McNickle v. Phillips Petroleum*" and "Preventing Sexual Harassment in the Workplace" and "The Long and Winding Public Policy Road of *Burk v. Kmart.*" Dry stuff, even to a lawyer, so Pat Cremin did his best to get through it by acting like he was at a Dean Martin roast. He was tolerably entertaining. But lawyers are by nature competitive beasts. So this need to be hilarious spread to the other speakers, and the net effect was that the TCBA labor law seminar ended up being as tiresome as amateur night at a Milwaukee comedy club.

After the introduction, the first thing Cremin said was, "You should've said, 'Let's get ready to rumble!' " One-upping poor Bill Wilkinson from the start. And then spent the next fifty minutes telling war stories. This constituted his lecture on sexual harassment.

Jim Priest spoke next and did his usual weird spiel, wearing, for some reason, a New York Yankees cap with his white shirt and tie, and throwing out Tootsie Pops to the people who answered his questions. Very Machiavellian. Looking and acting like a clown in front of lawyers he would not hesitate to drive a stake through in litigation.

Then there was a pleasant woman from Crowe and Dunlevy who felt the need to use props: decoys and little bathtub rubber duckies. Something about the importance of having your ducks in a row.

The last speaker was Carol Macy. She spoke about "Ethics in the Courtroom." She was pretty cool though; no lame jokes from her. Said the basic things lawyers and judges say about ethics—avoid conflicts of interest, keep a separate client trust account, you're never fully dressed unless you're wearing a smile—and so forth. Then she spoke about what, in her experience, juries responded favorably to. This part was interesting. She said that juries were starting to show more sympathy for plaintiffs than they used to.

This led to a true story about how Tulsa insurance lawyers had previously been spoiled by too many defense verdicts. During the insurance bar salad days, she'd run into Bill Smith, a partner in one of the more respected insurance defense firms in town. Carol asked him how it was going, and he said he'd had a bad week. He'd tried a case in front of a jury and they had awarded the plaintiff—ready?—six thousand dollars. He was genuinely depressed, she said.

Then she talked about how employment law was changing, and how juries responded to employment cases. Not surprisingly, she said, emotions could run very high in making these decisions. If a company dumped one of its employees after twenty-five years of loyal service, a jury was likely to punish that company regardless of what the law says. But it cut the other way too. Juries could well ignore the law that requires the employer to make reasonable accommodations to the employee with the disability and sympathize with the employer who doesn't want to spend the money on building a wheelchair ramp. Or keep a man on the job dying of AIDS. For many of these juries, they don't care what the law says; they're just going to do what they think is fair.

Carol took questions then. A plaintiff's lawyer named Tom Bright said, if he understood her correctly, she was suggesting there were some cases you were better off trying before a judge than a jury. Carol said that was right. And the AIDS disability discrimination, unfortunately, could be one of these cases. Family Medical Leave Act (FMLA) could be another one. The bottom line is, she said, you can change a law, but changing people's minds is something else.

Sitting amongst the other lawyers, Kessler thought of Clarence Darrow defending Leopold and Loeb. They had confessed to kidnapping and murdering a young boy. The city of Chicago wanted them executed. Darrow pleaded his clients guilty and took the decision to execute away from the jury. Then he convinced the judge to spare his clients' lives. It was a simple but brilliant strategy and it undoubtedly saved the boys' lives. And the parents of the young murderers rewarded Darrow by stiffing him on the fee. Poor bastard; he'd forgotten Lincoln's sage advice: always get the cash up front.

He put his attention back on Carol. She looked good. Smart, professional. Very cool. The Honorable Carol T. Macy. His . . . what? Girlfriend? Lover? Mistress? It had been six weeks since they first slept with each other. Six weeks of . . . what? Perpetual bliss? Well, not exactly that. But some good times. Some laughs, good conversations, great romping sex. So what were they to each other? Affairees, if there was such a thing? Should he even think about it? Whatever it was they had, they didn't talk much about it.

Carol took her last question, thanked the audience and smiled as the lawyers applauded her off the podium. Bill Wilkinson reclaimed the post, said something flattering about Carol and then launched into what he considered the most important employment case in the last five years. Which Kessler had never heard of.

He watched Carol as she walked to the back of the room and stopped by the sign-in desk. He stood up and began walking toward her. She was wearing a blue dress, conservative but flattering to her form. It stretched nicely across her hip as she bent over to sign something. Kessler wondered if he could get away with walking up and laying his hand on that hip. Just briefly. No one would notice. But then if he did that, would he be able not to kiss her on the neck?

He walked closer. He could smell her Dolce & Gabbana perfume now.

Howard Bengs got to her first.

Oh, shit. Howard fucking Bengs.

Senior partner in Harrison, Bengs, and Duvall, a medical malpractice defense firm. A gross man. Kessler had dealt with him once and hoped never to do so again. Not that he feared his prowess as a trial lawyer, though Howard was good, having the advantage of being without conscience.

A friend of Kessler's once had a trial against Howard. In the middle of it, Howard turned to the judge and said, "Your Honor, plaintiff's counsel just called me a 'fucker.' I ask that he be sanctioned at once." This he declared in front of the jury. Kessler's friend hadn't said anything to Howard. Howard made it up.

When Kessler had a case against him, Howard told him his

client was "just a fat Indian." The client's wife had died while in the care of a surgeon represented by Howard. He'd left a clamp inside her. At trial, during his closing argument, Howard warned the jury about the dangers of questioning God's will. The judge sustained Kessler's objection, and ordered Howard to drop the references to God. Howard went on to do it two more times anyway.

As a rule, Kessler made it a point not to befriend too many attorneys opposing him in trial. After all, there would always come a time when there would be hard feelings. Trials are adversarial and a friendship could get in the way of dutiful advocacy. During litigation, the blood would inevitably get up. But it almost always cooled down after it was done. He didn't really hate the lawyers he fought against. He was not, by nature, a hater.

But Howard Bengs tempted him. He brought out what Kessler's mother used to call "the occasion of sin." A desire to see harm befall another human being. A bully and a prick who took pleasure in inflicting cruelty on the weak and the poor. And an unprincipled liar to boot.

Now here was Howard Bengs shooting the bull with Carol Macy, his lover and intimate friend. Schmoozing Carol, asking her how Sam was doing. He'd run into Sam at the golf course, and he said the funniest thing. And Carol said, did he? And so on.

Kessler caught her eye.

She nodded at him. *Later,* she was saying.

Kessler retreated dutifully.

She came to his house that night. It was a Wednesday night. Sam stayed Wednesday nights in Oklahoma City, for reasons she never really explained. Sometimes, he would travel to Dallas on weekends. He liked to go to Kansas City, too, gamble on the riverboats. It was legal there. It was then that she and Kessler would get together.

She didn't kiss him on the mouth or cheek when she came into his house. She never kissed him hello. That wasn't particularly her style. She was a professional, wasn't she? Yet tonight, for the first time, he found himself missing the convention, missing the affection.

Carol poured herself a glass of wine, lighted a cigarette, and leaned up against his kitchen counter. Kessler thought about fixing a glass of whiskey, but then decided against it, leaving himself adrift without a drink in his home.

She said, "What did you think of the seminar?"

Kessler shrugged. "It was okay."

"Do you do much employment law?"

"Not too much."

He didn't say anything else. His back was to her as he washed knives and forks in the sink. He was in a poor mood and he was not sure he wanted to talk about it. Something on his mind, and his back was to her and he was communicating something to her even if he didn't intend to.

Carol said, "Howard Bengs."

She seemed to know he was thinking about it. She could be good at that sort of thing sometimes.

Kessler said, "What about him?"

"He's such a bullshitter."

"To say the least," Kessler said. He turned to look at her. "What did he want?"

"He wants to chair the Committee to Reelect Carol Macy."

"What did you tell him?"

"I told him it was fine."

Kessler turned off the faucet and leaned back against the sink.

"You did?"

"Yeah." A hint of defiance in her tone. Like, what of it?

Kessler said, "You're letting Howard Bengs chair your reelection committee?"

"Yes."

"Howard Bengs."

"Yes, Paul, Howard Bengs," she said. "What's wrong with that?"

"Oh, I don't know."

"What, Paul?"

"I don't know."

"No, come on."

"Well, Carol, he's a pretty sleazy man."

"Wait a minute, it actually bothers you that I would let him chair my reelection committee?"

"Yes, it bothers me."

She was smiling at him now. "Why?" she said.

He felt patronized by her smile and he had to tell himself to cool it.

"Because he's Howard Bengs—I mean, do you know the man?"

"Yes, I know him very well. Do you?"

"I know him well enough."

Carol shook her head, a woman addressing an adolescent. "No, you don't."

"Look, it's not just me that thinks this way. It's a rather universal perspective. Ask any lawyer that's dealt with him."

"Paul, don't be childish." Carol said, "It's not a question of whether or not he's not 'cool' enough. We're too old for that."

Oh my, Kessler thought. Steady, buddy, steady. Not the time to get angry.

"I'm not talking about whether or not he's cool," Kessler said. "He's dishonest and disreputable."

"So he's immoral?" She was still smiling at him.

"Oh, shit, I'm not talking about his personal life. I just know how he practices law."

She seemed to study him for a moment. And her expression was not a pleasant one. She said, "I see. I forgot that you were a principled man."

He sensed it then. No mirth in her tone when she spoke, the conversation shifting into something ugly now.

Kessler said, "What's that supposed to mean?"

"I mean that you are screwing a married woman. So maybe it's not a good idea to be throwing stones."

"I don't think I am." Kessler said, "And what does what you and I are doing have to do with anything?"

"I'm just saying you're awfully quick to throw out the judgments for someone doing what you're doing."

It knocked him back a bit. "What?" He said, "First of all, it's what we're doing. Second . . . look, I don't think either one of us is in the same ethical category as Howard Bengs. What we're doing is . . . it has nothing to do with the work."

"Oh, Jesus Christ," Carol said. "Has nothing to do with the work? What sort of line is that? It's adultery. It's deception. I don't care, myself. It is what it is. But I'm not going around calling other people sleazy. And I'm not going to pretend that I'm better than the rest of them."

"I think we're going off track here," Kessler said. "I'm only saying that Howard Bengs does not have a reputation for being an ethical lawyer. Because of that, I just think that you should think seriously before deciding to let him officially run your campaign."

"Have you ever run for public office?"

"You know I haven't."

"Then don't lecture me on how to run a campaign, okay? Anyway, you're wrong. Howard's aggressive, but he is not unethical. The only people who say that about him are the people who've lost to him."

Kessler looked at her for a moment before speaking, wondering now how well he knew her.

"I didn't lose to him, Carol," he said.

"Oh, here we go," she said, her voice raised now. "You and your goddamn ego. It doesn't ever occur to you that someone might be a better lawyer than you. Or more successful. No, you've got it all figured out. If they're winning, they must be dishonest and dishonorable. Not competent or formidable, or, God forbid, smarter than you. Oh, no. That couldn't be possible."

"Where is this coming from?" Kessler said. "I'm talking about Howard Bengs and you attack me?"

"Goddammit, we're not talking about Howard Bengs," Carol said, her voice raised almost to a shout. "We're talking about me. I've got a career, Paul. A political career. Howard Bengs is very influential in the defense bar. He's going to line up other firms like his to support me. I can't turn him down. I can't. Do you understand that? Do you have the slightest comprehension of political reality? Who are you, what are you . . . what have you accomplished that's so impressive that you think you can stand there and judge me? A sole practitioner who can't even get hired by a decent firm."

It silenced him.

Kessler liked being a sole practitioner. He did not envy anyone working for a big firm. In fact, he believed he was better off—professionally and, in a good year, financially—than most attorneys his age who were junior partners in the local, blue-chip firms. But that sentiment was beside the point. Arguing about it was beside the point. This woman he had been intimate with, who he had made love to, had just called him a loser, and she seemed to sincerely believe he was one.

Kessler said, forcing calm into his voice, "That's enough,

Carol. All right? Let's not talk to each other this way."

"You just called me a whore," she said.

"A whore?" Kessler said. "My God, what is the matter with you? I never called you that. I was speaking out of a concern for your welfare."

"My welfare," she said. "My welfare. Jesus—You're concerned about my welfare. To hear you say that just makes me want to throw up. Paul, all you care about, *all* you care about, is how this affects you. Oh, my girlfriend is married to dirty, corrupt Sam Clay. My mistress is letting herself be pimped by Howard Bengs. It's all about how it affects you. Do the bargains I've made in my life disappoint you? Have I 'let you down'? Well, tough shit. I'm not here to earn your bullshit schoolboy admiration. I'm not yours to judge. And you're in no position *to* judge."

He stared at her in shock, while she glared back at him. And there followed one of those depressing long silences when the mood is raw and all the feelings have been laid out and exposed, and people wish for a time machine to take them back a few minutes, before things got ugly and people said things they later liked to say they didn't mean.

Kessler thought, how did this happen? How did he and Carol Macy go from how was your day to My Lai massacre in the space of five minutes? How did it get so gross so quick?

How did it *end* so quick?

Because it was the end, and they both knew it. This was not going to be the sort of fight that ends with an emotional "I'm sorry" and "I was a thoughtless asshole" and "no, it was my fault" and so forth, followed by hugs and kisses and fierce copulation. There would be no makeup hey-hey. Too much structural damage for that. The ship's engineer was on deck now, telling the captain they'd all be underwater inside of an hour.

"Well," Kessler said, "I guess this is it for us."

"Right," Carol said. "Go find yourself a nice, simple girl. It's what you're looking for." She said, "It's what you can handle."

Kessler shook his head, trying to comprehend when the Pazuzu demon took over this woman's body. "Why don't we say good night," he said, gesturing her to the door.

"Fuck you," she said, but started to go. She didn't stop and turn at the door. She just threw the comment out with her back to him and kept walking.

"Stick to the car wrecks, Paul," she said. "You'll never survive outside that arena."

He found himself shaking his head again, reeling. "All right, Carol."

And closed the door behind her.

He was relieved when he saw her car back out of his driveway and heard it accelerate down the street.

He said aloud, "Well, that was awful."

He hoped he'd never see her again.

He would though.

EIGHT

She hadn't expected to see his car in the driveway. Wednesday nights, he was usually gone. But tonight his car was in the driveway.

They lived in a eight-year-old house in South Tulsa in a subdivision with an English-sounding name. The other houses were built quickly, using the same architectural plan. The lawns and the landscaping of the different homes varied, though, as people spent time and effort and money creating something they could look at, something they could care for. Neither Sam nor Carol did any gardening. They hired it out. Carol Macy looked at the brown Crown Victoria with the chief's plates. Shit, she thought. Not tonight. Not tonight.

Sam was in the living room watching Larry King on television. George Clooney was the guest, talking about his remake of *Funeral in Berlin*. Jesus, Sam was actually interested. Sitting there with a can of Busch beer as Clooney told Larry King he had not watched the original with Michael Caine because he did not want to be influenced.

Carol looked at Sam and felt the inevitable dread of coming home to him. She had been feeling that for a long time.

The television was positioned to the right of the fireplace. It was a modern raised fireplace with no mantelpiece. There was a rectangular red brick base.

She threw her bag on the chair and took off her coat. She walked by Sam without saying anything, went into the kitchen and poured herself a glass of wine. She came back to the living room and leaned one shoulder against the wall.

She said, "What are you doing here?"

Sam Clay said, "What?"

"I thought you were in Oklahoma City."

"No. I had to stay here tonight. There was a fund-raiser for Sheriff Glanz. At Southern Hills. I had to be there." Sam said, "I thought I told you about it."

"You didn't."

Sam kept watching television. The chief of police watching Larry King. Carol remembered thinking that he was an interesting man when she had first met him. But at home, he watched an awful lot of television. He would watch anything so long as it was on television. Like an old woman.

Carol took another look at him, and thought, the hell with it. She took a couple of files out of her bag and started for the stairs. Before she got there, he stopped her.

"Carol?"

She turned to him.

"What, Sam?" Making her voice tired.

"Where were you tonight?"

"I worked late."

"No, you didn't."

"What is this, an interrogation?"

"Are you having an affair?"

"Oh, not this shit again," she said. "Sam, why do you do this?"

"Are you having an affair?"

"Yeah, Sam, I'm having an affair. I met a nice sales clerk at the grocery store and I've been fucking him in the alley behind the courthouse." She said, "I'm going to bed."

God, she thought, what next? What the fuck next? She began to climb the stairs. He stopped her as she got to the landing.

"Paul Kessler doesn't work at a grocery store."

Her back was to him when he said that, and that was good. Carol had time to put on a face before turning to him. She drifted back into the living room and sat down. She wanted to show him she was curious and conversational. If she ran now, he'd know.

"Paul Kessler, the lawyer?"

"Yes, Carol. Paul Kessler the lawyer."

"The one in the parking lot, that day?"

"Yes, Carol."

"I hardly know him," she said. "I haven't seen him since then."

"That's not what Howard Bengs says."

Carol sighed, as if to say, all right, Sam, I'll play along. "What does Howard Bengs say?"

"He said he saw you two together at the seminar."

Carol traced over the labor law seminar. Impossible. She hadn't even spoken to Paul there. They exchanged glances, and that was that. What could Howard Bengs have seen? There was nothing to see.

Nothing to see inside the building.

But outside . . . oh, shit. Paul had walked her to her car, the dumbass. Said, "See you back at the house." The idiot. Him, with his antiquated let-me-walk-you-to-your-car propriety. And as she pictured getting into her car now, she could just see Howard Bengs in the distance getting into his Cadillac.

Why would he tell Sam? Why would the miserable bastard do that?

She said it. "Why would Howard tell you something like that?"

"Actually, he didn't," Sam said. "I saw him at the fund-raiser. And he told me how he'd run into you. And how smart you were. And how respected you were. And how beautiful you were. Said this young lawyer followed you around like a puppy dog. Still attracting the young men, huh?"

Carol said nothing.

"See," Sam said, "he thought he was flattering me, letting me know my sweet wife was still desirable. He didn't know he was humiliating me. He really didn't. If he did, I'd've killed him."

"Oh, Sam," Carol said. "Stop being so dramatic. You've never killed anyone in your life."

"Don't talk that way to me, Carol."

"I'll do what I want." Then she saw something in his expression that she didn't think she'd seen before. A darkness, an alienation. It disconcerted her, but only briefly. She said, "Look, Sam, he walked me to my car, okay? Maybe he's looking to get laid, but I really doubt it. He's a nobody. There's no affair."

Sam studied her for a moment. He was a policeman and he listened like one. Who was it that had said, there is no affair? *Is,* not *was.* There is no affair. Clinton. He had said it to dodge a question from Jim Lehrer. His Clintonesque wife.

Sam said, "So it was Paul Kessler."

It took Carol a little while to put it together, but she put it together. He hadn't known that it was Paul Kessler at the TCBA. Howard had only told her it was a young lawyer. He had tricked her.

Sam said, "When did it start?"

"Sam," she said, "we are not having this discussion."

"Yes, we are, Carol."

"No, we're not."

"Yes—"

"*We are not having this discussion, Sam,*" she said. "Do you know why? Do you? I'll tell you. Because I know, Sam. I know. I know about the whores. I know about Cassy's. I know it all. It's too small a town, Sam. The courthouse bailiffs are cops, and they talk and sometimes I hear. I hear them laughing at me because my husband is fucking whores. So don't talk to me of humiliation. Don't you dare do that."

Sam said, "How dare *you?* How dare you accuse me of something so disgusting. So vile—"

"Oh, stop it, Sam. Stop it." Carol said, "Your public service Holy Moses shit isn't going to work on me. You want answers, okay, I'll give them to you. Yes, I fucked him. I did it. And do you know why? Because you drove me to it. You, with your accusations and your fucking paranoia. Your absolute conviction that I was sleeping with another man drove me to sleep with another man. Happy now? Your sick fantasy is fulfilled."

"You—"

"What? Whore?" Carol said, "Why don't you just go ahead and say it, Sam. You've always thought that about me. You think all women are whores. You can't tell the difference, can you? Did you ever think that a woman might want to fuck a man because she actually enjoyed it?"

Sam Clay had heard his wife use the word *fuck* before. But as an oath, never as a verb. He had never heard her talk dirty. She had never said "fuck me" or "we fucked." Now she was using it in its real sense. Using it to torture him, to abuse him.

"Stop it."

"Because she might enjoy being pleasured? By a man."

Sam stood up, trembling. "You better stop that," he said. "You better—"

"Or what?" Carol said. "You'll divorce me? File it. File it and I'll hire Sam Daniel and you'll lose that fat pension of yours once we start getting into your filthy habits. You might even go to jail, you pathetic whore-fucker."

Sam grabbed her by her shirt front and pulled her toward him. "Stop it, stop it!"

She reached up and scratched his face, drawing blood. There was a sound from someplace, a look of recognition in Carol's eye. And he hit her. Hit her with the open butt of his palm. She screamed and fell back and hit her head on the base of the fireplace.

Then she lay still.

Sam heard himself say, "I'm sorry I did that. But you shouldn't talk to me that way. I'm sorry." He said, "Here, I'll help you up."

But she didn't move.

"Carol?"

She remained still.

And that was when he first thought he might have killed her.

He thought it again, a couple of seconds later, when he heard a man say, "I think she's dead, Sam."

Sam whirled to see Lieutenant Vannerson behind him.

Sam stood there shaking.

Van walked over to Carol's body and felt for a pulse. Then said it again: "I think she's dead."

NINE

Almost midnight. Buddy Matlock and Ray Miller sitting in an unmarked Ford Taurus. Still. Tedious. The quiet only broken by the unraveling of McDonald's cheeseburger wrappers. Fast food in a parked car. A stakeout.

Buddy said, "You hear about Jeff?"

Ray said, "Dennison?"

"Yeah."

"I heard something about it," Ray said. "OC sprayed a guy?"

"Yeah," Buddy said. "IA's goin' after him."

"You're shittin' me."

"No," Buddy said. "They're talking about giving him sixty days on the ground."

"Sixty days without pay?"

"Yeah."

Ray said, "For what?"

"He arrested a guy," Buddy said. "DUI. Handcuffed him behind his back. They take him back to the station, put him on the bench in the booking room. Well, the turd starts yelling at everyone there. I'm gonna sue you . . . and you and you. Jeff tells the guy to shut up, but he keeps yelling. Then he starts screaming he's gonna fuck Jeff up the ass, kill his family, and what have you. Jeff walks over to the guy, like, you know—I warned you—OC spray in his hand, and before he even gets to him the turd points his head down to the ground. Obviously, he's had some experience with OC spray, knows what's coming.

Well, that's not good enough for Jeff, so Jeff grabs him by the hair, pulls his head back and sprays him in the nose and eyes."

After a few moments, Ray said, "That's it?"

"Yeah."

Ray said, "And they're talking about giving him sixty days?"

"Yeah."

"That is fucking bullshit," Ray said. "I mean, that is bullshit. When I worked shift with Sergeant Craddock, he did the same thing about twenty times. Never tried to hide it either. Nobody even investigated him."

Buddy said, "It's not what you know, it's who you blow."

"What's the brass got against Jeff?"

"Well, you know Jeff," Buddy said. "He's active in the FOP union [Fraternal Order of Police]. Likes to push the union rights. Maybe too much. Between you and me, he files grievances on things I wouldn't mess with. This is their chance for a little payback."

"Ain't that illegal?"

Buddy said, "Probably."

Across the street, the front door of a house opened, and a man came out. He walked around to the side of the house and picked up a trash can. Then he carried the trash can to the edge of the front yard, past the blue BMW in the driveway, and set it down.

Ray said, "Is that him?"

Buddy Matlock studied Paul Kessler walking back into the house. "Yeah, that's him."

"He stays up late."

"He's going to sleep sometime," Buddy said. "Until then, we wait."

Ray said, "And after he goes to work?"

"We come back."

TEN

Driving to work that morning, Kessler tried to put it out of his mind. But the ugly scene of the previous night kept replaying itself. And as it did, his thoughts were at times melancholy and at other times simply gross. It was at those angry times that he told himself to stop it. Told himself to stop being bitter, to will it out of his mind.

Where was it going to go, anyway? It was only an affair. He couldn't have believed he would one day marry Carol Macy, could he? Hadn't he known that all along? That for all their education and elevated discussion of trials and case law and courts and other lawyers, they were probably just two bored, lonely, horny people using each other. Hadn't she known that he'd known? He told himself that may have been the explanation for the blowup. Then told himself, screw it, he didn't know what she thought and probably never would.

He turned on the radio. AM 740, John Erling saying that the people in Oklahoma City were just laughing at us Tulsans, laughing, because we hadn't yet built a downtown soccer arena. Kessler turned the radio off.

He'd been with other women. More often than not, the relationship would simply fade away, and with the passage of time, they'd gradually become friends. Not close friends, but at least a stage where the other would be glad to learn of the other's good fortune. That's the way it usually worked. For him, knock-down, drag-out fights were rare. He doubted he'd remain friends with Carol Macy.

Kessler's office was on Fifteenth Street. It was a two-story house that had been converted into offices. He co-owned the building with Jack Feld, a divorce lawyer and former law partner. They rented out the remaining spaces to other attorneys. The other lawyers included Mel Watkins, a sixtyish oil and gas man; Barbara Woodward, a smart and accomplished family lawyer, who kept mostly to herself; Mace Mills, the young hotshot; and Ron Battles, a guy who'd inherited a pile of money and seemed to work about fifteen hours a week.

Then there was the private investigator, Hank Patterson. Former Noble County sheriff's deputy and insurance investigator.

They were conservative people mostly, with families and mortgages and minivans. Not exactly the zany collection of personalities you see on a David Kelly sitcom. But then no law office is like that.

Jack's and Kessler's sole employee was Jeanne Calvano. She had been Kessler's secretary from the time he started practicing law in Tulsa. She was a good-looking woman. Dark, thick hair and one of those curvy, smooth figures that might be seen in an old Italian film. She was married to a firefighter and had an eight-year old son. She was twenty-nine years old.

Kessler walked into the reception area. Jeanne was on the telephone. Today, she wore a black skirt and a short-sleeved brown sweater.

She was saying, "No, we did not agree to pay half of the court reporter's bill . . . Yes, I am sure . . . uh-huh . . ."

She looked up at Kessler and smiled.

He smiled back and picked up his messages out of his message slot.

"You're certainly welcome to try . . . okay, you do that. Bye-bye."

Jeanne hung up the phone. She said, "You've got another one." She tore a message strip off her pad. "Barney Stokes. Potential bad faith insurance claim."

Kessler couldn't resist it. "Kicking ass and taking names, huh."

Jeanne rolled her eyes and Kessler started walking.

She called him back. "Hey."

He turned to see her motioning him back enticingly with her index finger. She liked to tease him that way sometimes, knowing he liked it.

"What?"

She placed a cardboard box on top of her desk. "Candy bars. Two dollars apiece."

"What for?"

"Travis's soccer team."

He shook his head and reached into his pocket and pulled out a ten-dollar bill. "Soccer moms," he said. "You're all fascists. Well, give me five of 'em."

He walked by Jack Feld's office. Jack's door was open. He was on the telephone. Jack was a divorce lawyer, or "matrimonial lawyer" as he called himself. Kessler waved to him, then threw one of the candy bars on his desk. Jack waved back and Kessler walked on to the break room.

It was a law office break room like any other. Bunn coffee maker, sink, small table, and counter space. On the refrigerator was a *Far Side* cartoon: a dog lawyer arguing on behalf of his dog client to a jury of twelve cats, "Is this the face of a cat killer? Cat chaser maybe. But, hey, who isn't?"

In the break room he found Hank Patterson and Mace Mills. Mace slouching up against the counter, telling Hank how he'd just slayed 'em yesterday at worker's comp, Hank quietly tolerating it. The morning bullshit over a cup of coffee ritual.

Hank Patterson was a tall, thin man in his early forties. He still wore the thick cop's mustache and expensive, polished cowboy boots, jeans, and a sportcoat. He was quiet with people he didn't know well, and he retained the slightly intimidating air of the steel-boned redneck who would inflict serious harm if provoked. He was one of those timeless sorts of people that you could easily imagine being an 1849 frontiersman. He was Kessler's closest friend.

Mace Mills? Picture young Paul Newman as Fast Eddie Felson in *The Hustler* and you're halfway there. He had that kind of shit-eating, I-been-waitin'-a-long-time-for-this, Fatman grin. Add an expensive wardrobe, tailored suits he probably couldn't afford. He'd been out of law school for only a couple of years. Intelligent enough and very confident, but not the most diligent lawyer in town. He had guts though, had hung his own shingle after spending one year at the District Attorney's Office. He wasn't afraid to try an area of law he didn't fully understand, which was sometimes good and sometimes bad. Mostly, he paid his rent on time. Kessler liked Mace, in spite of himself.

Kessler said, "You boys got any work to do?"

Mace said, "I was just telling Hank about my trial yesterday."

"You'll never guess," Hank said. "He won it."

Mace said, "Do you want me to start over?"

"No," Kessler said.

He did anyway. Something about a work comp judge, one of Governor Keating's appointees, threatening to suppress his Rule 20 report because it had been written by a chiropractor. And Mace threatening to appeal it to the panel, and the judge backing down, and the insurance lawyer calling him "a young man with no respect for the forum" or something, but he won despite such overwhelming, crushing odds. Kessler decided to believe it.

Then Mace said, "Man, where were you last night?"

Kessler said, "Home."

"You should have come by Arnie's," Mace said. "I was there with a couple of lovelies; I could have used your assistance. We work well together."

"Yeah," Kessler said, "I make an excellent Jerome to your Morris Day."

"What?"

"It's a movie from the eight—never mind."

Mace said, "I thought you said you were coming."

"I never said I was coming," Kessler said. "I said, 'I'll see.' "

"We're a team, man," Mace said. "Say, when are you and I going to form a partnership?"

"Oh . . . God."

Hank laughed.

"Well," Mace said, "we can talk about that later. But you should have come last night. What else did you have going on?"

"Nothing."

Mace turned to Hank, shaking his head, gesturing to Kessler. "He'd rather read some history book than chase women. What do you do with someone like that?"

Hank, the ex-cop, regarded Kessler. He said, "Everything all right?"

Kessler said it was.

At his desk, he returned Barney Stokes's call, found out the guy's claim probably had some value, so set up an appointment for the next day. Then he began work on an ADA (Americans with Disabilities Act) case he wished he'd never taken. Like most lawyers familiar with the subject, Kessler had learned that the odds of winning an ADA case were roughly the same as filling an inside straight in poker. You could bust your ass getting it past a summary judgment, only to have a jury zero your client simply because they don't have much sympathy for whatever disability the person has. In this case, the client had been diagnosed with bipolar disorder. Kessler had no doubt the diagnosis was legitimate, but he feared a jury would unfairly conclude his client was just plain hard to get along with. Still, Kessler liked the woman he was representing and was determined to give her her day in court.

He ate lunch in his office, then left to mediate an auto negligence case in Broken Arrow.

In most federal cases, the courts will order the parties to attend mediation; some would say only because federal judges wanted to clear their dockets, and that was more or less true. But it can be a healthy process. The mediator is usually a federal magistrate, sort of a junior varsity federal judge. He or she is typically willing to tell the parties something they don't want to hear. They'll tell the plaintiff that there's a good chance they'll get nothing from the jury. And if they do manage to get something, the defendant could tie it up for years in appeal. Then the mediator will walk across the hall and tell the defendants, listen, with these facts, you could get socked for a million in punitive damages because that's what juries will do if they get mad enough. And so forth.

The mediations were nonbinding; neither side would be forced to settle the case. But at least half the time, they would.

Other mediations were not court-ordered. They could be scheduled by the parties on their own accord.

The case that was being mediated today fell into the second category. And it was Kessler who had, as coyly as possible, suggested it to the insurance company's lawyer. Asking for mediation was something he rarely did. He suspected most opponents would take it as a sign of weakness, a lack of faith in his case.

And truth be told, he did lack faith in this one. Cliff Forsman, his client, had been T-boned at an intersection at Utica and 41st and suffered a dislocated shoulder as a result. The driver of the other car had probably run a stop sign and had been given a traffic citation. So far, so good. But there were problems on the horizon. First of all, Cliff was a pretty difficult guy to like. He tended to get surly and defensive when he was stressed, like, say, during cross-examination. And there was a witness who said he thought Cliff had been going fifteen to twenty above the speed limit.

That's what the insurance lawyers knew. What they didn't know, yet, is that about one month after the collision, Cliff was arrested for passing a bad check at a Homeland Grocery store. Now, passing a bogus check has nothing to do with whether or not a party was contributorily negligent in a car wreck. But it does, arguably, go to credibility. And there was a good possibility that, one, the insurance lawyer would find out about it and, two, the judge would say it was fair game for cross-examination. And if that happened, the jury in this civil case could dispense its own form of rough justice and punish the criminal a second time with a crap award. Or none at all.

It took a few hours. The mediator wasn't as aggressive as Kessler would have liked him to be. Consequently, it took more time than it should have to talk Cliff down from his quarter-million-dollar mountain. Finally, Kessler asked to be alone with his client so he could tell him what he was up against.

"Cliff," Kessler said, "I'm not going to sit here and say, 'Let's go to trial and we'll get a hundred thousand!' when I honestly believe the odds of it happening are slim to none. Don't get me wrong; it could happen. But it isn't likely to. That jury finds out you passed a hot check, we're hosed. It's that simple. As of now, the insurance lawyer doesn't know you were arrested. You haven't lied about it, because you don't have to volunteer information harmful to you. You only have to answer the question before you. But whether or not you're asked if you've ever been arrested, he will find out. The good ones always find out about that sort of thing. And when he does, he's going to call me up and say, 'Paul, that forty-thousand settlement offer I made last week? Well, now it's twenty thousand.' And I can play tough, tell him to fuck off, say, see you at trial. But then we'll be left with a judge and jury who may well give you a lot less or nothing."

Cliff said, "You said we shouldn't take less than fifty."

"I said that before you got arrested, Cliff. That changed things." Kessler said, "Look, let me make something clear. Let me make something very clear: I don't think you should get less money because you got arrested. I don't judge you for that. Shit, I've bounced checks. I don't think it's fair that you should get less because you had the bad luck to get caught doing that. But what I think doesn't mean anything. The value of the claim is not what I think it's worth. It's not what you think is fair. It's not even what the insurance company thinks is fair. *It's what the jury thinks is fair.* Now I can't look you in the eye and say a jury is going to be as understanding as . . . well, they should be. I'm not going to mislead you about that. I have to warn you about what can go wrong. You just don't know what can happen at trial."

Cliff stewed for a few moments. Then said, "It's just bullshit, though." And Kessler knew then Cliff was thinking about it. He better.

But then Kessler remembered the cardinal rule of lawyering: never judge a client. You won't change anyone, and they'll only resent you if you try. Perhaps for good reason.

Kessler said, "I know it is, Cliff. But it'll be done. Listen, if you take the forty thousand today, I'll cut my fee to twenty-five percent. You'll pocket thirty thousand. If we go to trial, by contract, my fee's going to go up to forty percent. Forty percent of fifty thousand is twenty thousand, which would leave you with . . . thirty thousand."

Cliff shifted in his chair; the idea appealed to him. But he was hesitating about something. He finally said, "Well, I don't want you to get shorted."

Kessler said, "Don't worry about me, Cliff."

Lights flashing. Blue, red. Blue, red.

Kessler glanced up at his rearview mirror.

"Shit," he said. Now what?

He pulled the BMW over, onto the grass next to the road.

He was on East 145th Street, just outside of the city limits. Fields on both sides of the road. It was dark now.

Kessler took his driver's license out of his wallet and prepared to hand it to the police officer. He didn't think he'd been speeding, but you never knew about these quasi-country roads. You were apt to forget you weren't on a highway and pump it up to seventy without thinking.

He heard the cop's voice in the distance, loud, "Step out of the car, please."

He did and found himself in the glare of a spotlight.

He put his hand up to shield his eyes. And then the spotlight went off.

The cop said, "Just stay there for now."

Kessler thought that was unusual. He liked to drive fast, so had had his share of traffic stops. Usually, one of two things happened: either the cop walked up to your door, you remained in your seat while he stood next to the door, told you what you did wrong, and wrote you a ticket; or, the cop asked you to come back to his patrol car, you sat next to him in the front seat while he told you what you did wrong, and wrote you a ticket.

But this guy told him just to stand next to his own car, and to stay where he was.

The driver's doors to both cars were open. Kessler stood in

front of his, while the cop stood behind his.

Kessler said, "Was I going too fast?"

The cop said, "Yeah. You were."

Kessler said, "Well, what—"

But he stopped. A car drove by, its headlights on Kessler's back, on the cop's front. Then it was past.

Something. A movement by the police officer. A flash of something, near his waist. It made Kessler step out and move farther away from the door of his car.

Kessler held up his hands, chest level. "I'm not armed," he said.

The policeman said, "What?"

"I'm not armed."

The cop said, "I know."

A couple of confused and then ominous moments passed. Kessler said, "Then why have you pulled out your gun?"

The cop didn't answer. He just stared at Kessler. And Kessler thought he'd seen that stare before. He'd never seen the man before, but he'd seen that expression before. He'd seen it on the faces of men just before they shot a deer.

Kessler stared back.

A deer in the headlights.

Slowly, Kessler stepped backwards toward the car.

And the cop stepped out from behind the door of the patrol car, arm extended down, gun at the end of it. Now raising it to waist level . . . and Kessler turned and ran, and there was a shot, Ray Miller not thinking it out, not realizing that if he just stood still and planted his feet he could fire a clean one through the runner's back, but just firing from the hip, as they say, and missing the prey completely, then firing another one through the open door of the BMW . . . and Kessler was inside the car now, shoving it in first and stomping down on the accelerator, and shots were coming into the back of the car now, *thoonk*,

thoonk, and he kept his head low, the engine crying out for second gear, and Kessler lifted his head up to look out of the windshield in time to see that the road had curved, heavily, and he was now in the oncoming lane and there was an oncoming truck, and there was no time to scream, just crank the wheel right, back into his own lane, correcting it too much and putting a wheel into the ditch, as he sat up and struggled to keep the car on the road, and he almost succeeded when the right tire hit a rock and the car slid into the ditch, and sank down to a level position.

He estimated that he'd only driven a couple of hundred yards. Just a matter of time before the fucking lunatic ran up here and shot him. The car was level, but it sat in soft mud. The tires spun forward and then backward. No movement.

If he took the patrol car, he would later be asked why he didn't radio in a shots-fired call right after the shots were fired. *You were in the car, why didn't you radio it in?* And he didn't know how he would answer such a question. He didn't even know how Van would be able to answer that one.

That was the main reason Ray stayed on his feet when he went after Kessler.

But there was another reason, one that he wasn't even fully aware of, buried beneath the conscious mind. And that was simply the love of the hunt. The love that exists in most men and hasn't quite been washed out by 2,000 years of Christian civilization. Ray Miller wanted to track down his prey and kill him.

He rounded the bend in the road and saw the BMW almost immediately. Thankfully, that truck hadn't hit it. If it had, it might have killed the lawyer. But then it might not have. And then there would be other police units and fire engines and paramedics. In short, it would be a clusterfuck.

The BMW was still running. But there was no one inside.

Using his flashlight, Ray found the footsteps in the mud leading out of the ditch and onto the road. He looked over to the other side. Nothing but another ditch and a fence behind it and an open field behind that.

Amateur, Ray thought, as he climbed out of the ditch and began to walk across the road. Take a twelve-year-old from back home and he'd be able to track this fellah down.

He found the lawyer lying on his stomach in the other ditch and put the flashlight on him.

Kessler stood up. He decided he would speak because he feared if he didn't he would go to pieces. He needed something. And maybe if he talked long enough, another policeman, one who wasn't insane, would come along and he could place himself in his custody.

So they stood there for a few moments. The cop standing in the road, the lawyer in the ditch below.

Kessler said, as calmly as he could, "I suppose I should have tried the field."

Ray Miller shook his head. "You wouldn't have made it," he said. "Full moon."

"Are you really a cop?"

"Of course."

Kessler said, "Why?"

It was the calm way that Kessler asked the question, like he was only curious, that made Ray hesitate. Had the man begged for his life or screamed out "don't" like most men would have, Ray would have plugged him on the spot. But the question was asked in a simple and dignified manner. The guy seemed to be telling Ray he understood it was nothing personal. And suddenly Ray felt the guy deserved some dignity, deserved to know.

He would meet his maker soon enough, but he deserved to know.

Ray turned the flashlight off and put it in his belt. Then, using his left hand, Ray pulled a transparent plastic bag from his jacket pocket. Inside the bag was a .38 Smith & Wesson snubnose with a cherry-wood handle.

"Recognize it?"

Kessler studied it briefly. Then more closely. Finally he said, "It's too dark."

"Well, it's yours," Ray said. "See, you tried to use it on me."

Kessler ordered himself not to panic. It wasn't happening; it couldn't be happening. The automatic was in the man's right hand, so Kessler edged to the right, so the man would have to turn. He said, "Why would I do that?"

Ray shook his head, as if to say, we've talked too much. He'd given the man some explanation, but now the man was trying to stretch it, take advantage of his hospitality.

Kessler spoke quickly. "Okay," he said, "just tell me this: is it about the chief's wife? Can you at least tell me that?"

"Yeah," the cop said. "It's about the chief's wife all right." Kessler could hear the smile in the man's voice.

Kessler moved forward. "Well, let's talk about it then. Why would you get yourself into this mess for him?"

"Stay there."

Kessler edged farther, and Ray backed farther into the road. "Are you in trouble? We can talk about it."

A rumble in the road.

"Stop right there," Ray said. "You're the one in trouble."

"I just want to talk," Kessler said, and bolted right.

Ray was conscious of two things at once: one, the man running away from him, to his left and, two, a vehicle on the road, to his right. To take a shot at Kessler, he had to turn even farther left, putting his back to the oncoming vehicle. He could squeeze off one round, but then would have to move out of the road . . . because then—

He miscalculated.

The truck hit him square in the back, smashing his vertebrae and knocking him down like a bowling pin, bashing the life out of him. He may or may not have died instantly, but he was certainly dead by the time the truck got finished rolling over him.

The driver of the truck was not even aware of Ray Miller until he'd hit him. He braked after the impact. It took another fifty yards to bring the eighteen-wheeler to a stop.

Kessler came out of the ditch, walked over to look at the dead cop. His first thought was to stay there with him and wait for the truck driver, and then wait for the police to arrive. He almost did. But then he saw the plastic bag on the ground with his gun in it, and that changed his perspective. He walked over, picked it up, and put it in his coat pocket. Then he crossed the road and got into his BMW. Gently, he released the clutch while pressing down on the accelerator, pretending there was an egg between his foot and the pedal that he didn't want to break. The car edged forward, then slowly moved up and out of the ditch and then down the road.

ELEVEN

Kessler lived in an older house in the Zinc Park neighborhood. The house had a garage at the end of the driveway that was not attached. Kessler parked the BMW in the garage, and got out and looked at the bullet holes in the trunk of the car and the damage to the undercarriage. The car was not totaled, but there was several thousand dollars' worth of damage.

How would he explain this to the insurance adjustor? Damaged while fleeing homicidal cop. He took another curious glance at the holes in the trunk, turned off the garage light and left.

In the house, he did his best to keep from shaking to pieces. He fixed himself a whiskey, sucked it down, and then fixed another and decided he would only sip at it. He sat in the den in his leather chair.

On the table next to him sat the glass of whiskey and the gun in the plastic bag. It was his all right. A Smith & Wesson snubnose with a wooden handle. He had bought it from a friend of Hank's last year. It was unregistered and he usually kept it on a shelf in his bedroom closet. He'd checked when he got home and it wasn't there. No, it was in this plastic bag.

So . . . he thought, this should be easy. Someone took it from his house, probably today, and had given it to the cop that tried to kill him. A . . . what? Frame? For what?

Who would want him dead?

Well, maybe Carol Macy. She'd been awfully mad when she

left the previous night. But that was too flattering. Carol goes and gets a cop to kill him? Absurd.

But then nothing was making any sense right now.

Sam Clay. Sam Clay found out about the affair and decided he would have him killed. What was it the cop had said?

Yeah, it's about the chief's wife all right.

But there was something more. The guy had almost laughed when he said it. Like Kessler didn't get the joke.

What was so funny?

The chief of police of a major metropolitan city decides to have a man killed because he's fucking his wife? It didn't make any sense. It was barbaric. Sam Clay was not the Count of Monte Cristo; he was a public official. A *manager*, for godsake. People like that don't try to kill you when you cross them; they just try to get you fired from your job or get you in trouble with the state bar.

And even if murder was justified on some bullshit Southern code of honor level, why wouldn't Sam Clay do it himself?

Oh Jesus, he'd fucked up. He should've stayed out there and waited for the police. He could have kept the gun in his pocket. Or explained it to the police somehow. But he should have stayed. He should have called Hank. Hank used to be a cop; he would have known what to do.

Hank.

Kessler picked up the phone and dialed his number.

Hank's wife, Bobbie, answered.

"Hi, Bobbie. Hank in?"

"Hey, Paul," Bobbie said. "No, he's at the boys' basketball game. He's coaching Ted's team this year."

"Oh, that's right. I forgot."

"You got his cell number, don't you?"

"Yeah. I got it."

"But he's liable to have it turned off during the game." Bobbie said, "You know how he is."

"Yeah, I know," Kessler said. "All right, Roberta. I'll talk to him later."

"Bye-bye."

"Bye."

Boys' basketball, bullshit, Kessler thought. I'm worried about going to fucking jail. He stared at the telephone for a few moments. Then stared at the gun. He thought, take your mind off it. Just for a couple of minutes. And then you'll be able to think more clearly. Distract yourself. Then decide whether or not you should call Hank.

He turned on the television and surfed. The NBA semifinals, then Larry King, then movies he'd mostly already seen. Then the early news on the local Fox channel. And there it was.

Our top story tonight. Tulsa County District Court Judge Carol Macy is missing. Members of her staff telephoned the police this afternoon after she failed to show up for work. Judge Macy is married to Tulsa Chief of Police Sam Clay. Lieutenant Jennifer Liu said the police are investigating her disappearance. Chief Clay offered no comment, but has asked for our prayers.

Kessler turned to look at the gun on the table.

Yeah, it's about the chief's wife all right.

Smiling when he said it.

Kessler walked out to the garage. He opened the door, walked in and closed it behind him. Then he turned on the light.

The holes in the trunk seemed to stare at him. Black holes. At least, they should be black. But they seemed to be light underneath.

Slowly, he moved forward. He placed the key in the lock and opened the trunk.

Then placed his hand over his mouth. To stop himself from screaming or vomiting or both.

Carol Macy's body, wearing a gray Burberry overcoat, was lying in the trunk of his car.

TWELVE

Jennifer Liu, police spokeswoman, stood on the front steps of the downtown police station and told the press that all they knew at the present time was that Judge Macy was missing. They didn't know anything else.

A reporter asked, was the chief worried?

Well, of course he was worried, Jennifer Liu said. He's her husband . . . No, we have not received any contact from kidnappers . . . No, I repeat, no contact from any kidnappers . . . of course, it's possible, any number of things are possible, but it doesn't seem likely that she was kidnapped.

Jennifer Liu gestured to another reporter. In her gesturing hand was a can of Diet Coke, the acknowledging finger extending from the top.

Are you telling us that she's just taken off? That she's run away?

I don't think that suggestion is appropriate at this time, Jennifer Liu said. To question the state of their marriage is both unfair and unprofessional.

Isn't it possible that she just went on a vacation and forgot to tell him?

Jennifer Liu looked at that reporter for a couple of seconds, then gestured to another one.

We're not questioning the state of their marriage per se, the other reporter said, we're just wondering if she's left him?

Jennifer Liu didn't see the distinction there, but she did say that Carol Macy was a district court state judge, not some flighty waitress or young girl. If she wanted to end her marriage, she wouldn't just disappear. She wouldn't run away. But again, it's not appropriate for us to get into such things.

There was some laughter and rumble among the press.

And Jennifer Liu, being earnest, told them that she did not at all mean to suggest that waitresses were irresponsible or reckless. Which only brought a little more laughter.

Toward the back of the crowd, a reporter turned to his cameraman and said, "Run away, bullshit. If she hasn't been kidnapped, she's dead, man."

A political consultant once told Sam Clay, "When you speak before a large group of people, try not to be too wed to the text of your speech. What I mean is, don't *read* your speech. When you read your speech, you sound like a kid in school reading his term paper. Worse, really. Don't worry if you don't say the words exactly as they appear on the page. A speech is not a play. Just be natural and your message will get through."

Sam sat at his desk, preparing it.

I've just received a call from Lieutenant Vannerson. My wife has been killed.

No. "My wife" is too impersonal.

I've just received a call from Lieutenant Vannerson. Carol has been killed. Murdered apparently. They found her in the trunk of a car owned by a man named Paul Kessler. We don't know much about him now. He was pulled over in a routine traffic stop by one of our officers whom he attempted to shoot. The officer returned fire and killed him.

Then what? Leave it at that?

No. He'd have to add something.

I don't know what else to say. She was everything to me.

Walk off, let Jennifer take over. They wouldn't want to ask

him questions after that. Not then. They would simply sit back and admire his courage and respect his grief.

And then it would be over.

He looked at his watch. A little after eight o'clock. He should receive the call by now. The officer in the anteroom outside his office would buzz him and say it's Lt. Vannerson, and he would pick up the call and say, what? Oh, God, oh my God, no. More or less the words he'd actually uttered twenty-four hours earlier. Then make the slow walk to the microphones outside.

The telephone buzzed about fifteen minutes later.

"Chief," Jennifer said, "it's Lieutenant Vannerson."

"I'll take it." Then, "This is the Chief."

"Sir, Lt. Greg Vannerson. Sir, I've got some bad news."

"Yes?"

"We've got an officer down near a Hundred and forty-fifth and Bowman."

A moment passed. Then another moment, the chief wondering if he was missing something.

"What? What did you say?"

Van said, "I said we've got an officer down on a Hundred and forty-fifth Street, near the Bowman intersection. He's dead, sir. I know this is not the best time, sir, but policy requires that the chief be notified every time an officer is killed in the line of duty."

Chief Clay said, "Yes, that's right, lieutenant." In a voice he tried to make the same, he said, "What happened?"

"Officer Ray Miller was hit by a truck, sir," Lieutenant Van said. "Probably killed him instantly."

"Is that . . . is that it?"

"Yes, that's all we can determine at the present time."

Chief Clay closed his eyes for a few moments, then opened them. He said, "How . . . ?"

"I don't know, sir."

Chief Clay said, "Who's there with you?"

"Deputy Chief MacDougall, the shift supervisor, about a dozen other officers." Van said, "Paramedics, a fire engine."

"Put MacDougall on."

"Chief, MacDougall here."

Chief Clay could tell that the man had been crying.

"Mac, I'm sorry to hear about Raymond," the chief said. "Did you know him well?"

"Not very," MacDougall said. "A young cop, Jesus. Any time an officer falls . . ."

"I know. Mac, what happened?"

"Hard to tell, sir." MacDougall said, "The radio car's about two hundred yards down the road. His service weapon has been fired. Several times. But we haven't found any of the rounds yet. The driver of the truck, he didn't see anything. Why he was standing in the middle of the road, we just don't know."

"Had he radioed anything in?"

"No, sir, he did not." MacDougall said, "It appears he was chasing someone on foot, and fired his weapon at them. We haven't found any evidence of another weapon being fired, but we'll have better luck with that when the sun comes up. He hadn't radioed for backup, so whatever happened, it must have happened quickly."

"Right."

"Probably chasing someone on foot, and didn't see the truck coming."

"Right."

MacDougall's voice cracked again. He said, "It's just a fuckin' shame, is what it is."

"I know, Mac," the chief said. "I know. Let me speak to Lt. Vannerson again."

Van said, "Yes, sir."

"I want you to call me soon. On a direct line. In about five minutes. Do you understand?"

"Sure."

The phone rang approximately four minutes later.

Sam said, "Where are you?"

"On a land line," Van said. "Inside Wendy's."

"Alone?"

"Yes."

Chief Clay said, "Would you tell me what the fuck is going on?"

"I don't know what happened," Van said. "He must have pulled the guy over and then lost him. His weapon's been discharged."

"I know that. How could he . . . ?"

"Miss?" Van said. "I don't know. He chased the guy on foot, apparently, and then got hit by a truck. Just bad luck."

"Bad luck? Is that what you call it?"

"Sam, calm down," Van said. "Where's the guy going to run to? He's not a flight risk. He lives here. He works here. He's a homeowner. He's not going anywhere."

"You say that after someone just shot at him."

"He's a lawyer, Sam. Men like that put all their faith in the system. If he finds . . . the thing we're talking about, he'll probably call the police."

"It would be better if you found him before that."

"I understand that," Van said, pushing his voice, "but a phone call to the police won't solve his problems. He has no way to tie this to us."

"No way to tie it to you, Van," Chief Clay said. "But I was married to her."

"I know you were, Sam." Van said, "But . . . listen, just don't worry, all right? I'll call you in a couple of hours."

"What are you going to do?"

Van thought, not run everything by you beforehand, that's

for damn sure. Sam couldn't think straight. And Van was not a man to be micromanaged, not a man to seek pre-approval for all his decisions.

"Sam," he said, "I'll call you in a couple of hours."

Thirteen

The Grand Lake of the Cherokees covers approximately ninety square miles. It is manmade, created in 1940 when they built a dam across the Illinois River by a town named after Walt Disney. It's a long, twisting lake, with several coves and tributaries, with a length of thirty miles as the crow flies, and stretching to a width of three miles near the middle. About 1,300 miles of shoreline, with depths of up to 750 feet. Though not breathtaking in its beauty, it is scenic enough. Nice enough for a weekend getaway if you own a cabin and a boat, though probably not worth the trip if you don't.

It was where Kessler decided to dump Carol Macy's body.

He hadn't much time to think about it. And he didn't have the time to sound out his options with Hank Patterson, and he wouldn't have even if he did have the time. Essentially, there were only two options:

Get rid of the body; or,

Call the police.

Why not call the police?

Sitting in his den, next to the telephone, he thought about it. He stared at the telephone like it was a thing possessed, tempting him and terrifying him.

The phone seemed to say, call the police. Call the police and tell them what happened. Tell them to come out to the house and give them your explanation. Then call Martin Kelly, criminal defense attorney, and ask him to come out too. Or, call Martin Kelly first. That would be the sensible thing to do. Under normal circumstances, under normal . . . circumstances.

And then what?

An arrest. Then a trial. Then the task of constructing reasonable doubt. The State's burden to prove guilt beyond a reasonable doubt, but for all intents and purposes, his burden to show reasonable doubt was there. And what would the State have? Carol Macy, dead of a head injury, lying in the trunk of a car belonging to a man she'd had an affair with.

Framed, you say? And who framed you? The police? Rriiiighht.

How many times had he read of, had he heard of, cases claiming the infamous Police Conspiracy and discarded every one of them?

There was that one filed in the Eastern District, where Johnnie Cochran and Barry Scheck alleged that the Ada police department had framed that poor schmuck Williamson for the murder of a young girl in order to protect a drug trafficking ring involving, yes, Ada police officers. Kessler had read about that one and thought, good fucking luck proving that, boys. Who would believe that? Yeah, the Ada cops and local prosecutors had almost sent an innocent man to lethal injection. But it was just a fuck-up. The cops had just made a mistake, that's all. Police conspiracy? Come on.

Nor did he believe that the Philadelphia police had framed Mumia Abu-Jamal for the murder of police officer Daniel Faulkner. No matter how fervent the protests of Susan Sarandon and Alec Baldwin and a good portion of the citizens of France, anyone who took the time to analyze the evidence would know that Abu-Jamal had killed Officer Faulkner in cold blood. It was what the evidence showed. It was what any reasonable person without an agenda would have to believe.

He did not believe the LAPD framed O.J. Simpson. He did not believe the Oklahoma City police conspired to cover up a rape in the Glitter Dome scandal. He did not believe the Cincinnati police targeted the black community for genocide.

He had always been skeptical of claims of police conspiracies. A sensible man had to remain skeptical of such claims, didn't he?

As he considered it now, he wasn't sure why he'd been so dismissive. Perhaps because they'd all seemed so fantastic. Perhaps because the lawyers alleging the conspiracy theories more often than not seemed like nutballs. Perhaps because he didn't think police officers could be clever enough to pull off such conspiracies. Perhaps it was because he just didn't want to think American police officers would do it even if they could.

It was these thoughts that presently consumed him and depressed him, and to a degree, even shamed him. He, the plaintiff's lawyer, the defender of the little man, the challenger of State Farm and Tulsa Regional Medical Center and other large, powerful institutions . . . he had just always presumed cops just wouldn't do that. He believed. And because he believed, because he had believed, he knew that if he were on the jury, he'd convict himself. He could see himself now, taking delight in teasing one of the local coffee shop liberals. *Police framing a car wreck lawyer? What sort of Oliver Stone bullshit is that? What do you think this is, the Soviet Union? Go back to France with all the other anti-American lunatics. Oswald acted alone.*

"You just don't know what can happen at trial."

He had said that, *Christ,* not three hours ago. But three hours ago was a thousand years ago. Before his nice little world had been turned upside down. *You just don't know what can happen at trial.* No, you really don't.

The thing was, these guys *were* clever. They had taken steps. Someone had killed Carol Macy and then set about to frame him for it. No getting away from that. The cop on 145th had meant to kill Kessler, and then place Kessler's own gun in his dead hand. Then, *voila,* dead murder suspect on the ground with dead Carol Macy in the trunk of his car. That was the plan. Neat and simple.

So, that meant the cop or someone else had broken into his house and taken his gun. Probably while he was at work today. And Carol Macy? God, probably resting in his trunk since last night.

Call up the police and explain it to them. *See, they had this plan* . . . watch them nod their heads, humoring him.

Well, that's interesting. But why were you running from a police officer?

The police officer was trying to kill me.

Well, okay, but you had this gun, *your* gun, pointed at him. And a dead body in the trunk of your car.

And he would say . . . he would think of something to say . . . he made a living out of saying the right things at the right time, didn't he?

But he didn't know what he would say then.

While they followed up with: do you see where that leaves us, Mr. Kessler? With four. As in, two and two makes.

They liked things like that. They liked two and two to make four. District attorneys liked things neat and simple too. And it would be a headline grabber. Nice young white lawyer of some prominence, killing a judge that he was sleeping with. Change a few names and stick it in next week's "Law & Order." Sex, murder, lawyers in love, Jesus, the newsworthiness of that. National headlines.

Regarding the option of going public, there was only one thing that gave him hope: the framers had decided to kill him. That was the irony. It gave him some, for lack of better word, *comfort* to know that they'd tried to kill him. Because it showed that, whoever they were, they weren't willing to take a chance on having a trial, even if Kessler was the named defendant. They wanted him dead.

But it wasn't much comfort. It wasn't enough. In the end, Kessler decided they were just trying to be thorough. Yes, framing him for the murder of Carol Macy was probably a pretty good idea. But framing him and killing him was a far better one. Had it worked, he wouldn't be around to cry "Police Conspiracy" to any jury. It would be an open and shut case.

Opened by who?

He almost said aloud, "Well, I know I didn't kill her."

And then he thought, hey, fuck 'em. But then he realized, he *had* said that part aloud. "Fuck 'em. Fuck them. Murderers." He had said it loudly and with real anger, and rather than taking it as a sign that he was losing it, it strengthened him, emboldened him, moved him out of the den and into his bedroom where he took off his jacket and tie, and put on jeans, hiking boots and a black sweater, still feeling the tight fear, but using it, channeling it.

Fuck these pricks. One part of their wonderful plan had just fallen apart. It had been run over by a truck, and was now lying in a dead, bloody heap. Let the pieces of shit scratch their heads over that for a few hours. While he took apart the rest of their plan.

It was that or wait for them to make their next move.

FOURTEEN

What was it they said? You're not paranoid if they really are out to get you. Kessler reminded himself of that as he drove the old Route 66 highway to Grand Lake. The interstate would have been quicker. But there were tollbooths on the interstate, and tollbooths had cameras. Didn't they? Well, maybe they did and maybe they didn't. But why take chances. People were out to get him, see.

At Vinita, he turned west onto highway 60 and took it to highway 85. Soon he crossed a shallow bridge and was winding his way onto Monkey Island. It was mid-May, a good two weeks before Memorial Day, and there was very little traffic. It was approximately one in the morning when he reached Jack Feld's cabin.

He had been to the cabin several times before. Jack had a party there every summer for his office mates. Lots of kids and dogs and water skiing. Not really Kessler's cup of tea; too much commotion and heat. But tolerable once a year. He was not cut out for water sports, and the idea of owning a boat made him ill. A bigger nuisance he could not imagine.

There were exceptions to this antipathy. During the fall and the spring, he liked lakes like this one and cabins next to them. It wasn't too hot, and the evenings could be pleasant. And to throttle a boat full out over still water as the sun set was to live life. The times when you could actually do that were rare. After Memorial Day, most weekends would find Grand Lake packed with boats and Jet Skis, heavyset guys with coolers full of beer playing Van Halen or something else to remind them of their lost youth, the water churned up and choppy and the sun beating down mercilessly. There were people who liked that sort of thing. But for Kessler, it was only worth the trip when it was empty and peaceful. And a little bit cold.

The cabin sat on a dirt road with four others, spaced about thirty yards apart.

Kessler stopped the car, turned off the ignition and sat quietly.

He looked at the other cabins. No lights on. But that didn't mean no one was home. There were people who retired and sold their first homes and then simply moved into their cabins. Jack himself had spoken of doing it, if his wife would allow it.

Was anybody here?

He made himself sit in the car for ten minutes. Then, seeing no overt sign of activity, he got out and walked around to the deck behind the cabin. He found the spare key under the second potted plant and let himself in through the back door. He went into the kitchen.

On the refrigerator was a crudely drawn picture of the cabin and the boat, four stick figures next to it: Mommy, Daddy, and the two little girls. Sally, Jack's five-year-old, had drawn it.

Scumbag, Kessler thought. You're a fucking scumbag. A good friend lets you use his cabin a couple of times and you take advantage of him. Break into his home and steal his boat. Adultery, hiding evidence from the police, and now this. He thought briefly of a higher power and silently asked, what do you want from me? Then he took the keys to the boat off the peg next to the refrigerator.

He walked back out to the car and thought, now the hard part begins. He stood behind the trunk and listened. Crickets, night sounds, the woods. He was alone. He took a deep breath and opened the trunk.

Her body was wrapped in a rug that he had taken from his living room. He slung the burden over his shoulder, shut the trunk, and carried the body down to the dock. He set it on the dock next to the slip that held Jack Feld's red and white Chris-Craft boat. He took the tarpaulin cover off the boat and put the body behind the rear seats. Then put the tarpaulin over the body.

He walked back to the car and opened the trunk again and took out one of the gray cinder blocks and carried it out to the boat. Then did the same with a second cinder block.

After he untied the boat from the dock, he turned the key to the ignition. The sound of the engine cracked into the night and he forced himself not to look at the shore to see if any house lights came on. He kept it under ten miles per hour until he got out of the cove, then pressed the throttle down full to take the boat out to the deep center of the lake.

It was when he reached the center of the lake that he felt truly alone. Lights on the shore barely perceptible and the only sound was the water sloshing against the hull of the boat. He took the body out of the rug and tied her legs and feet to the cinderblocks. He found that while he was doing this and other things, he had to just . . . remove himself from it. Remove himself from the horror of it. He remembered that she had told him she was a Catholic. They buried their dead, but they believed the body was nothing more than a body. The body was merely the host to the soul. It isn't her, he told himself. This thing I'm tying blocks to, this thing I'm desecrating and throwing into the lake isn't her.

Yet when he positioned her body on the side of the boat, he paused. He wasn't aware that he'd been sobbing or even crying, but his face was wet with tears. He said, "You didn't deserve this, Carol." He paused, then said, "You were a good judge." He realized how awkward that sounded after he'd said it and,

113

though he was alone, felt suddenly self-conscious. But he'd always respected her professionally even though it seemed strange to think of it now. She had been a very good judge. He said, "I'm sorry that I was angry with you, Carol. And I'm sorry that I—that I thought such unkind things about you. I'll—" He stopped. He would what? Try to be a better man? "Make it up" to her? Find her killers? Jesus God, he hadn't been thinking about that at all. He'd only thought about saving himself.

With that, he heaved her over the side.

FIFTEEN

He drove to Alva, taking highway 60 then 64 across the northern part of the state. Narrow, two-lane highways passing through a dozen small towns. He avoided the interstates, did not use the cell phone at all. Submersed into the night, maintaining silence.

He got there a little after 5:00 a.m.

The land was south of town, a twenty-acre spread with yellow prairie grass and enough trees to break the wind. There was a small white house and an old large barn that you could see through, and a steel shed that once housed a tractor.

Kessler pulled the BMW up to the steel shed, got out of the car, and opened the doors. He drove the car inside, got out and shut the shed doors behind him.

"Can I help you?"

A polite voice, but firm. Meaning, explain what the hell you're doing, partner, and now.

Kessler turned to see a man in his late sixties holding a shotgun. Not leveled at him, but there all the same.

Kessler said, "Don't shoot me, Dad."

Jim Kessler squinted in the dark. "Paul?"

Kessler resisted rolling his eyes. Honor thy mother and father, even when you're the only son they have. But Jim adjusted his sight to the dark and said, "What are you doing here?" Concerned, and right to be so.

Kessler said, "I'm in trouble."

Jim Kessler, sixty-six years of age, wrinkled and thin, but

tough in mind and body. Tough enough to deal with this. His expression was tired, but it betrayed no despair. None Paul Kessler had ever seen.

Jim Kessler said, "Why don't we go inside."

Paul's mother, Ellen, had died a year earlier. Aneurysm, sudden and fatal, like someone had just flicked her life switch to off. His father had chosen to stay on the farm, such as it was, in Alva. Paul had asked Jim if he wanted to move to Tulsa and live with him and Jim had stared at him, almost in pity, and said, "Don't you value your privacy?" And Kessler had answered that, yes, he did. And Jim had said, "Well, don't you think I value mine?" Cross-examined by the old man.

They were close, but not close. In his life, there had been few heart to heart father and son chats. And there was no resentment because of that. They were both independent men, solitary and quiet-natured. Paul had never felt he'd been denied anything. He had reserved his intimacy for his mother, and he had understood that Jim Kessler was very much a man of his time. A man from a time where men didn't gush with emotion over their sons, didn't scream and shout at their sporting events, didn't tell them they loved them, but demonstrated it every day in ways subtle and not so subtle.

Jim Kessler was seven years old when the Japanese bombed Pearl Harbor. He fought in the Korean War, returned home and took a job as an aircraft mechanic in Oklahoma City. Within a few years, he became active in supporting the formation of a union in his workplace. After one of the early pre-certification meetings, he and a friend were jumped by men hired by the company. The men went to work on them, using clubs and brass knuckles. Jim fought back, fiercely, protected his friend and put one of the goons in the hospital.

After that, the company filed criminal charges against him. Witnesses swore that Jim Kessler viciously and without provocation attacked "security guards" employed by the company. Two of the witnesses were men who had attended the union meetings, men he'd worked with and was trying to form the union for. Eventually, he met with the company owner and a local deputy sheriff. They told him if he left town, the criminal charges would be dropped.

That was how he and his young pregnant wife came to her hometown of Alva. Jim got a job as a mechanic at a garage, and eventually opened his own repair shop, and, after the baby was born, Ellen took a secretary's position at the local university. They got by, worked and saved, and then eventually prospered to a comfortable small town retirement.

Paul was a college student when he first learned about his father's union background and exile from Oklahoma City. His mother told him. He supposed, to some extent, that it had motivated him to go to law school. But he never did discuss it with his father, and his father had never discussed it with him. Jim Kessler was a private man and he wanted pity from no one. Still, to the son, it was an injustice unanswered. Being younger, he could not understand how the older man had made peace with it. But he had.

When Ellen passed, Kessler and his sister, Katy, stayed with Jim for a week. After that, Jim was free and emotional with Katy in a way he couldn't be with Paul. They shared their grief openly, while Jim and Paul were more likely to sit in the living room together watching television in silence. Katy returned to her own family in Austin, and Paul returned to Tulsa.

In the South, they say that you're not really a man until your father dies. That it's only then that you realize you no longer have to get the old man's approval. Nor can you seek his counsel. You can't rely on him to tell you what to do, and you don't have to worry about him bawling you out for not doing what you're told. And it's then that you know, for better or worse, you're truly on your own.

Perhaps that was true. But Kessler thought the same could be said when a man's mother dies. No more do you receive the unconditional love and support, the comfort that can only come from a mother. Not to mention her wisdom or strength. Maybe they had their own expression about mothers and manhood in New England. Who knew? He'd never lived in New England. There were passages in life and you simply endured them, whether you were a man or a boy.

He did not know why, but for some reason he did not find it especially difficult to tell his father about this godawful mess he was in. Perhaps it was physical and emotional exhaustion. Or a deeply human need to confess sin. In any event, he told him while they sat at the kitchen table and sipped coffee.

Told him, "I had an affair with a woman. She was married. To a police officer. To the Tulsa chief of police actually. I'm not going to tell you that it was okay or that we were in love, because it wasn't and we weren't. I did it and she did it and . . . well, it's what happened. Anyway. A couple of nights ago, we had this awful argument, very unpleasant, and she left. At that point, we were through. The next day, yesterday, she didn't show up at work. She's a judge. I didn't know this until last night. I mean, I knew she was a judge; I didn't know she'd disappeared. Anyway, last night . . . last night, I was driving home and a cop pulled me over. He gets me out of the car, I'm unarmed, I'm not threatening him in any way, and he tried to kill me. Shot at me. Why, I had no idea. I got away, he accidentally got run over by a truck, and it saved my life. He's dead now."

Kessler looked at Jim to see if he needed a breather. He didn't.

But he began to edit the rest of the story, take out parts. Not to mislead the old man, but because he didn't want him to ever become an accessory to any sort of crime, such as disposing of a corpse. Kessler said, "I found out a couple of hours later why the cop tried to kill me. This woman I had the affair with—the one who disappeared—she's dead. Someone killed her, murdered her. And now they're trying to frame me for it. And I guess it would have been easier for them to frame me if I were dead."

Jim said, "Who's involved in this?"

"Well, obviously her husband," Kessler said. "Others, of course. If I'm lucky, maybe it was just the one cop who tried to kill me. But I doubt it."

"Is the whole department dirty?"

"God, I hope not," Kessler said. "It's hard for me to think straight. It wouldn't make sense for an entire city police force to be on the take."

"Don't be so sure."

"Well, if that's the case, I'm hosed no matter what I do," Kessler said. "So I'm going to have to presume it's not."

"And you came here," Jim said. Though not resentfully. He just said it.

Kessler said, "I had no place else to go."

They were quiet for a few moments. Then Jim said, "You know what happened in Oklahoma City?"

"Yeah, I know," Kessler said. "Mom told me."

"I figured she had."

"Why didn't you?" Kessler said. "Tell me, that is."

"I knew you knew," Jim said. "I figured that was enough."

After a while, Kessler said, "Yeah, I suppose it was."

Jim said, "Have you been questioned by the police?"

"No," Kessler said, "but I think it's just a matter of time."

"What will you do then?"

"Lie."

Jim Kessler said, "Okay."

Kessler steadied himself. If he broke down now, the old man might break down. . . . No, maybe he wouldn't. The old man was strong, always had been, but there could be no show of panic. The old man had to believe that the son had a handle on things. He had made the old man a co-conspirator in this disgusting mess. He had pulled him in it and there was no time to feel shame over it now, no time to tell him he was sorry or seek his forgiveness or his approval. They were in it now and both of them had to be strong because otherwise they wouldn't survive.

Kessler said, "I think I know what to do."

"What about going to the attorney general or the FBI?"

"Is that what you'd do?"

"I don't know."

"See, that's my problem," Kessler said. "I don't know either. I don't know if that'd work. It might. It might get me out of this. But I'd be putting my fate completely in their hands. Completely. They might bust the police corruption case wide open. Or, they might interview a chief of police and a bunch of cops and conclude that I'm a lunatic, that I'm a murderer. A desperate man trying to escape intravenous injection." Kessler said, "Anyway, it's too late for that."

"All right, then," Jim said. "What do you want me to do?" Volunteering to help.

Kessler said, "I don't want you to do anything. Just leave the BMW in that shed, and don't let anybody see it. I'll take care of it later. And I need to borrow the car. Can you get by with the truck?"

"Paul, I haven't used the car since your mother died."

Kessler rubbed his face in his hands.

"You're exhausted," Jim said. "Why don't you go to bed." Telling him now.

"Okay," Kessler said, taking a sudden comfort in the order. "But I need you to wake me up in one hour. For this to work, I have to return to Tulsa as soon as possible."

Sixteen

Jim woke him at seven a.m., as promised. He changed clothes, put on one of his father's undershirts, a sweatshirt and a pair of khaki pants. He put his own clothing in a trash bag and twisted the top. Then he took a screwdriver out to the shed and removed some items from the BMW. These he rolled into a towel. He put the rolled-up towel and the trash bag into his mother's Buick LeSabre.

Soon, he stood with his back against the car, facing his father. Kessler said, "All right then."

Jim Kessler nodded and said, "Okay."

It was a gray spring morning. Chilly. Birds were chirping and in the distance there were cows making their wake-up sounds.

Kessler said, "It'll be all right, Dad. I'm pretty sure."

Jim said, "Well, you know who you are. I see that."

Which made some sense . . . maybe. Kessler smiled. "Well," he said, "that's something. I'll call you in a couple of days."

He reached out briefly and patted the old man's arm. Kessler men did not embrace. Kessler got into the Buick and drove down the trail.

As he neared the gate, he glanced into the rearview mirror to see Jim walk after the trail of the car. Tall and strong and watchful. Kessler rubbed his eyes for a few moments, rubbed himself and held on and succeeded in preventing the flow of tears. He drove on.

★ ★ ★ ★ ★

He stopped in Enid and threw the trash bag into a Dumpster behind a convenience store.

He made it to his house a little before 11 a.m. He undressed and showered and shaved. He brewed a pot of coffee and made some toast. Then got back into uniform: Brooks Brothers brown suit, Allen-Edmonds shoes, blue dress shirt, and dark green tie. Then he called Martin Kelly.

"Martin, Paul Kessler here. I need to retain you . . . no, for me . . . That's right . . . You know about Judge Macy's disappearance? . . . yeah . . . I was seeing her, having an affair with her . . . Yes, a sexual relationship . . . That's pretty much it, but I want to give a statement to the police, and I want you to be there when I do . . . No, I think this is the best way to handle it . . . I understand that and I appreciate it, but I think this is best . . . let's shoot for one o'clock, my office . . . No, I'll set it up . . . yeah, I'm sure. Okay then."

He placed his next call.

"Yes, this is Paul Kessler, I'm an attorney here in Tulsa. I need to speak with whoever is handling the investigation into Carol Macy's disappearance. Yes, I've got some important information . . . Yeah, I'll hold."

A few minutes passed. Then:

"This is Detective Gilvetti."

"Detective Gilvetti?"

"Yes."

"Are you handling the investigation into Carol Macy?"

"Yeah. Who am I speaking to?"

"Paul Kessler. I'm an attorney here in Tulsa. My office is Seventeen-oh-eight Fifteenth Street, near the Panera Bread?"

"What can I do for you?"

"I was involved in a relationship with Carol Macy, and I'd like to talk to you about it."

Silence for a few moments.

The detective said, "What do you mean 'relationship'?"

"We were having an affair."

Kessler heard the man exhale. He pictured the detective writing things on his pad and underlining them.

The detective said, "Can you meet with me today?"

"Yeah, I think that'd be a good idea," Kessler said, keeping it light. "Is one o'clock at my office all right?"

"Why don't you come down here?"

"No," Kessler said, "I've retained Martin Kelly, and he wants to do it at my office. Do you know Martin?"

Kessler heard the man sigh. Disappointed and then resigned. Gilvetti said, "Yeah, I know him."

"He'll want to do it at my office."

Detective Gilvetti gave it a shot. "How come you've hired a lawyer?"

"I'm a personal injury lawyer, a car wreck guy," Kessler said. "I don't know anything about criminal law."

"Yeah, but what do you need a criminal lawyer for?"

"Hey, ask Martin when you see him," Kessler said. "One o'clock then?"

The detective sighed again.

"Yeah, that's fine."

SEVENTEEN

Kessler made sure he was behind his desk before the interview began. Martin Kelly sat to his right. The detectives sat in the client chairs in front of the desk.

Detective Dean Gilvetti was a big man who looked more Irish than Italian. Dark-haired, but fair-skinned, with a heavy jaw and wide shoulders. His nose was a little red, a drinker or someone who spent his weekends outside.

The other detective was a smaller man with thinning brown hair and glasses. He could pass for an accountant with his crisp white shirt and knit tie. He was in his late thirties. He said his name was John Edwards.

Martin placed a tape recorder on the desk and switched it on. He gave the date and time and said this:

"This is Martin Kelly, attorney for Paul Kessler. Present in the room are myself, Mr. Kessler, and detectives Dean Gilvetti and John Edwards of the Tulsa Police Department. Detectives Gilvetti and Edwards are investigating the disappearance of Judge Carol Macy. It should be noted that at this date, her whereabouts are still unknown. The record shall reflect that Mr. Kessler contacted Detective Gilvetti on his own accord and told him about his involvement with Carol Macy and asked to give this statement and to be subject to any questions the detectives have. Paul?"

Kessler said, "If it's all right with you gentlemen, I'd like to tell you about my involvement with Carol Macy before you ask any questions."

Gilvetti tilted his face toward Edwards. Edwards looked up from his pen and pad and shrugged, and Gilvetti said, "Go ahead."

Kessler took a breath and began.

"A few weeks ago, I tried a case in Judge Macy's court. It was *Harris vs. Ellis.* I don't remember the docket number, but it should be easy to find out. I ran into Carol in the parking lot after the trial, she was with her husband, Chief Clay. I'll get into that more later. Anyway, a couple of days after that, I ran into her at a coffee shop. She sat down and we started talking and, well, next thing I knew, we'd agreed to meet that night for a drink. Now, I think at that point, we both knew we were beginning something. We didn't talk about what we'd do that night, but she said something about going to a place where we wouldn't run into people we know. So we met at a bar on the south side, called Tommie's. That would have been on the Saturday night, following that trial, if you want to check it out. So we met there, and, had a few drinks and then . . . then we went back to my house."

Gilvetti said, "Where was her husband that night?"

Kessler said, "Well, I don't know really. She told me he was out of town."

Gilvetti said, "Go on."

"That was how it started. We'd get together once or twice a week after that, usually at my house. A couple of times at a hotel."

"Which one?" Gilvetti said.

"The Residence Inn, on Yale."

"So," Gilvetti said, "it was a sexual relationship."

Kessler looked at him for a moment before answering. "Uh, yeah."

Then thought he saw the other detective smile to himself. That's the one to keep your eye on, he thought.

"It was a consensual sexual relationship," Kessler said. "Nothing . . . out of the ordinary, really. Just a man and a woman getting together. But it probably wasn't enough for either of us."

Gilvetti said, "What do you mean by that? Enough what?"

"Well, I mean, it really couldn't last," Kessler said. "To spend time with a woman, you need to be able to go out in public with her. Have dinner, see a movie, that sort of thing. The secrecy gets old after a while. It gets . . . confining. It gets lonely too, I suppose. I guess neither one of us had thought about that."

Gilvetti made a grunting noise.

"Anyway," Kessler said, "it lasted a few weeks. Then, on Wednesday, two days ago, I saw her for the last time. She'd given a lecture at a CLE seminar—"

"What's that?" Gilvetti said.

"It's Continuing Legal Education," Kessler said. "I was there too. Though I didn't really talk to her there. Later that night, she came over."

Gilvetti said, "Did you have sex with her then?"

"No," Kessler said, "I did not. We had an argument, and she went home."

"You say," Gilvetti said.

"I'm telling you what happened," Kessler said.

Gilvetti said, "What was the fight about?"

"It was not a fight," Kessler said, "it was an argument. We didn't come to blows or anything like that. But what was it about? Well, she said she was mad at me because she said I was judging her."

Gilvetti said, "She said you were judging her?"

"Yes."

"For what?"

"For letting a lawyer named Howard Bengs manage her campaign," Kessler said. "Her reelection was coming up. And I told her she shouldn't let Howard Bengs manage it."

"So you were mad at her for that?" Gilvetti said.

"No, I wasn't mad at her," Kessler said. "I was disappointed in her. I don't think Howard Bengs practices law very ethically, and I told her so. Then she said I judged her for staying married to Sam Clay."

Gilvetti said, "For staying married to Sam Clay?"

"Yes."

Gilvetti said, "That 'disappoint' you too?"

Kessler shrugged. "Yeah," he said, "I guess it did. I thought she could do better than Sam Clay."

Gilvetti sat up in his chair. He said, "When you say 'do better,' were you referring to yourself?"

"No," Kessler said. "No, she and I wouldn't have been a good match either. What I meant when I said 'do better,' was, do better by marrying someone she actually loved. Or even liked. Or do better on her own."

"So you fucked her for a few weeks," Gilvetti said, "and using your mastery of psychology, you determined she didn't love her husband."

Kessler paused. He put a clinical sort of frown on his face. Cold and dispassionate. He said, "Well, no, I'm not a psychologist. But, really, anyone with any sense could have seen what I saw. It was obvious."

Gilvetti said, "To you."

"Detective, I don't know the man," Kessler said. "I only knew her. He may be a great guy for all I know. But I do know she was very unhappy in that marriage. She initiated the affair with me, and I'm not even sure she liked me very much."

Gilvetti said, "And you resent her for that?"

"Resent her for what?" Kessler said.

"For using you," Gilvetti said.

"Using me?" Kessler smiled. "Oh, I think it's more accurate to say we used each other."

Gilvetti shook his head to show disgust. But Kessler could tell it wasn't sincere. He'd seen the trick used too many times by lawyers in depositions and court.

"Listen, detective," Kessler said, his tone patronizing the man, "I can fully understand your disapproval. It's not the sort of thing decent people approve of. And I can appreciate your loyalty to another police officer. But with all respect, I am helping you with your investigation."

"Never mind what you think are my loyalties," Gilvetti said. "Go on with your story."

Kessler shrugged again. "Well, there's not much more to tell. About her and me anyway. She left the house that night, and the next evening I saw on the news that she was missing."

Gilvetti said, "What time did she leave your house?"

"Sometime between nine and ten, I think."

Gilvetti said, "What did you do the rest of the night?"

"I stayed in."

"Anyone with you?"

"No," Kessler said. "I live alone."

Gilvetti said, "So you don't have an alibi."

"I wasn't aware I needed one."

Gilvetti said, "Don't get too confident, counselor."

"Well before you go down that path, detective, I should tell you what else I saw. I saw your chief grab his wife by the arm, roughly, in the courthouse parking lot. And when I went to see if everything was okay, he accused her of sleeping with me."

Gilvetti said, "Wasn't she?"

Kessler was aware of the silence in the room now, the detectives and Martin Kelly staring at him, blown away by it, a well-known judge having an affair with this guy. The big detective wanting to punch him, the smaller detective writing everything down and not saying a word, Martin Kelly, his jaw open, thinking that this would be on the front page of tomorrow's *Tulsa World*. They were waiting for it now.

And Kessler threw down the card.

"Not then," he said.

Kessler noticed the other detective still staring at him. Then he put his gaze back on Gilvetti. It would take a stronger man than this to break him.

Detective Edwards said, "Are you saying he drove her to it?"

"Like Mr. Gilvetti said, I'm not a psychologist." Kessler said, "She did tell me that he had made those sort of accusations before. That he had always been paranoid about it. She told me that I was the first man she'd had an extramarital affair with. And I believe she was being truthful."

"So if I follow you correctly," Edwards said, "she went to bed with you to punish her husband."

"Well, she never quite put it that way," Kessler said. "She just said the accusations hurt her and drove her crazy."

Edwards said, "Did she tell you she was afraid of him?"

"Well," Kessler said, "not directly. She was a proud woman. An attorney. A judge. She would never say, 'Sam scares me.' Or, 'I'm frightened of Sam.' But she did say things like, 'God, if he ever knew' or 'If he ever finds out, we're dead.' "

Edwards said, "She said, 'If he ever finds out, we're dead'?"

"Yes."

Detective Gilvetti did not like where this was going.

He said, "You know something, Mr. Kessler? I think you're a fucking liar. I think you're saying all this shit to protect yourself."

"Detective," Kessler said, "I don't give a shit what you think. All through this interview you've been trying to pin Carol's disappearance on me, using little tricks and innuendo."

"Paul," Martin said, his hand raised to stop him from saying anything more.

"Are you here to find out the truth?" Kessler said, "Or are you here to find someone to pin this on?"

"Paul—"

"You accuse me of protecting myself. Who are you protecting?"

Gilvetti leaned forward in his seat. "You got something to say, boy? Say it."

It was intimidating. He was a big fucking man, with a Glock .40 on his side. And right now, he looked like he had violence on his mind. He looked like he wanted to use a phonebook on Kessler's head, get a more respectful tone.

But what's he going to do? Kessler thought. Shoot me, then Martin, then maybe this other cop who may just be clean?

"Okay," Kessler said, "I will. I had no motive whatsoever to kill Carol Macy, and you know it. But your boss did. If he found out that she was sleeping with me, he had plenty of motive. I called you, detective. I called you. And I told you everything. Let me ask you something: this little interrogation, have you done anything remotely similar with Sam Clay? Have you asked him where he was the night she disappeared? Does he have an alibi?"

"As a matter of fact," Gilvetti said, "he does."

"Who?"

Gilvetti said, "I'm not here to answer your questions."

"Well, I'm through answering yours," Kessler said. "Like I said, I don't think you're looking for the truth. Martin, this interview is over. I'm invoking my Fifth Amendment right not to incriminate myself."

Gilvetti quickly stood up. "You think you're so fucking smart," he said. "But we're gonna find something on you, and you won't be so damn smug then."

Kessler felt his heart beating, as scared now as he had been in the middle of Grand Lake. But he could not panic, he had to play it through.

"I wonder what you mean by that, detective?" Kessler said.

"What are you saying?" the detective said.

"You know full fucking well what I'm saying. See if you can get a search warrant to search my house. But if you do, I'm going to have someone there videotaping the whole thing. You're not planting anything on me."

Gilvetti leaned forward and shoved Kessler's desk back on two legs and then let it fall to the ground with a moderate crash. Kessler remained in his chair, but Martin and Detective Edwards both stood up, Martin saying, "Hey, hey!"

Edwards put a hand on Gilvetti's arm. He said, "Let's go."

They left, the crash of the desk and the fear and threat still in the room afterwards.

Martin Kelly said, "Jesus Christ, in twenty-five years of practicing law, I don't think I've ever seen anything like it."

"Ah, fuck 'em," Kessler said. He pointed a finger at Martin. "Hey, you eaten lunch yet?"

"Uh, no," Martin said. "But I think we should talk about—"

"Martin, would you do me a favor and see if they've left the premises?" Kessler said, "I don't want them here bullying the staff with questions. Please?"

Martin was still staring at him. The scene and now Paul's cold tone.

"Yeah, okay."

It was only after he left the room that Kessler sank back in his chair, heaving a sigh of relief, wishing for a glass of whiskey, but remembering that he did not keep any in his office.

Eighteen

Mal Devereaux, captain of the detectives, said, "He accused you of trying to frame him?"

"Yes, sir," Gilvetti said, "he did. But I should add that it's not unusual for us to be accused of that. The penitentiaries are filled with turds saying they got framed."

"That's true," Devereaux said, "but this is . . . a little different. He accused you of trying to protect the chief."

Gilvetti said, "Yes, sir, he did."

Devereaux said, "He called you first, though?"

"Yes, sir."

They were in Captain Devereaux's office. Devereaux at his desk, detectives Gilvetti and Edwards sitting in front of him.

Mal Devereaux was a tall, slender man, middle-aged with salt and pepper hair. He had been in the Marines, but the experience wasn't something you could see at first glance. He did nothing to make himself look tough or imposing, and he almost never made reference to his military past. For him, it was in the past. And like most soldiers, he quietly held the view that men who talked too much about their military experience either still belonged in the barracks or were trying to compensate for some present inadequacy. Like many strong men, he allowed people to think he was a bit of a softie. It was a useful way to get people to drop their guard and help you that much more, especially when you wanted to nail them. There was a picture of Barney Fife on his computer mousepad on his desk. But it was

"Yes," Gilvetti said. "He was at a fund-raiser."

Devereaux said, "Was his wife with him?"

"No."

Devereaux said, "That's consistent with the lawyer's story, isn't it?"

Gilvetti said, "How so?"

Devereaux said, "She was at the lawyer's house while the chief was at the fund-raiser. The lawyer said she left his house between nine and ten. What time did the fund-raiser end?"

"Eight o'clock."

"Did the chief go home after that?"

"Yeah."

"So," Devereaux said, "let's consider three theories for now. One: she goes to the lawyer's house. They get in a fight. He kills her. Accidentally or intentionally, we don't know. He puts the body in her car, drives someplace to hide her body. Leaves the car nearby, goes back home.

"Two: she leaves the lawyer's house. On the way home, she's carjacked. Carjacker takes her someplace, rapes her, kills her, leaves her. Which reminds me: have we found her car yet?"

"No," Edwards said.

Devereaux said, "We have to find that car. Use all available resources. Now, three: she leaves the lawyer's house, drives home to the chief. They have a fight, chief kills her. Puts her body in her car, drives somewhere, dumps her body and the car."

Devereaux looked at Gilvetti and said, "Those are just three theories. We still don't know what happened, okay?"

Edwards said, "The lawyer said that she was afraid of the chief. Says she told him that."

"Yeah, I know," Devereaux said. "But that's pretty convenient for him, wouldn't you say? It's not like she can step forward to deny saying it."

135

"Yeah, it's convenient," Edwards said. "He'd obviously want to protect himself. But do you think we should check into it?"

Devereaux said, "You mean check into the chief? In what way?"

"Pattern," Edwards said. "With women, I mean. See if there's a pattern of abuse."

Devereaux thought for a moment. Then said, "We may have to do that. But hold off on it for now."

"Okay," Edwards said, looking at Devereaux for a moment. "For now."

Devereaux dismissed the men. He waited for the door to close. Then opened his desk to check to see if his tape recorder was working. It was.

Good Lord, he thought. Sam Clay a murderer? It couldn't be possible. But under any normal circumstances, he would be a suspect. The husband was always a suspect in cases like this. As a husband, he would have to be questioned. And by someone more competent than Dean Gilvetti. Someone with more guts. It would have to be done soon, too.

How did it get like this? he thought. It was once a good department. But in the last few years, something bad had set in. Bad karma. Men taping each other's conversations, a general aura of distrust, shitty morale. Good officers, men like Edwards, weren't being rewarded for their work. And bad officers just seemed to keep going up the chain of command, the bad pushing out the good. A failure of leadership perhaps. If so, he was partly to blame. And now, some wacko attorney crying conspiracy. Paranoid.

But whatever paranoia that guy was feeling, Devereaux thought, it was nothing compared to the paranoia of working in a police department. In times like this, you got to where you didn't trust anyone. You stooped to secret tape recordings of police officers you should trust, and who should trust you. But he didn't trust. He'd been in police work too long. He had seen too many internal disputes end careers. He didn't trust Gilvetti because he thought Gilvetti was dishonest. Not necessarily on the take, but dishonest enough to pin a crime on a man he thought deserved it. Say a lawyer who'd been fucking a cop's wife. He had to presume that everything he said to Gilvetti would be repeated, perhaps even to the chief himself. Count on him saying things like, *we've got a solid case against this turd lawyer, and what does Captain Devereaux want to do about it? Go after the chief.*

And, for different reasons, he didn't fully trust John Edwards. This was shameful to him because he liked and respected John. He thought John was a decent, honest cop. And a good detective. And, cynical as any twenty-year cop would be, he was genuinely moved when John had said, "I'm a police officer." Fiercely, proudly.

Well, why not? Goddammit, it was something to be proud of. You serve and protect. You uphold the law, you enforce the law. And if in doing so, you snag another cop, then so be it.

But he feared that John thought *he* was dishonest. John didn't try to hide the fact that he thought Dean Gilvetti was a piece of shit, and in that assessment, he was probably right. But Devereaux could tell that John hadn't yet made up his mind about him, Devereaux. And that was the sad irony: he couldn't trust John Edwards because he suspected John Edwards didn't trust him. As if the man still had some unanswered doubts, thinking: *And what about you, Captain Devereaux? Are you going to protect the chief too?*

No, he was not. But until this thing got resolved, he was going to be goddamn careful. He wasn't going to give anyone any reason to doubt his integrity. But he wasn't going to give the chief cause to end his twenty-year career either.

Devereaux picked up the telephone and dialed a number.

He said, "This is Captain Devereaux. I need to speak with the city attorney. . . . Tell him to call me back today."

The city attorney didn't return the call until the next day. He didn't seem too happy when he did.

NINETEEN

When Kessler had first moved to Tulsa to practice law, he had shared office space with Martin Kelly. They soon became friends in spite of their personality differences. Martin was about fifteen years older, and came from an upper-middle-class family. He was one of ten children, and had seven kids himself. He had been wild in his youth, a student activist at a time when campus protests took the form of burning down ROTC buildings. He eventually straightened out, went to law school, and learned to channel his inner angry young man into trial advocacy and coaching Little League baseball. Like a lot of men of his generation, the hippie that he had once been was hard to see. At least on the outside. He wore conservative suits and his hair was cut shorter than Kessler's.

Martin was one of the best criminal defense lawyers in the state. When he felt like working. He seemed to go in spurts. A few years ago, before his semiretirement, you couldn't turn on a television without seeing him, usually defending a client on a death penalty case. He knew how to use television better than Giuliani. He knew how to use it to tweak his opponents and get them to reveal strategies they otherwise wouldn't reveal. He was a natural showman. On one case, he responded to the then DA's mild criticism of him to a newspaper reporter by saying, "Real men try their cases in court, not in the newspapers." Consequently, what would have been a back-page story about a minor procedural dispute became front-page news.

Kessler didn't blame him for taking some time off. A death penalty lawyer spends his or her days trying to save the client's life. He doesn't use an operating room or medical procedures to do this, but writes and argues and appeals against a state that wants his client dead. It's the sort of work that takes its toll on the psyche.

But Kessler knew Martin Kelly had plenty of fight left in him. And he was fairly sure the man couldn't wait to get back in the news.

So after the cops left, they ordered in sandwiches and Kessler quietly went to work.

He said, "Well, what happens next?"

Martin said, "They'll search your house, your car, see if they can find anything. Since you didn't kill her, you should be all right."

Kessler said, "I didn't kill her."

Martin said, "I know you didn't."

Kessler shook his head, momentarily bewildered. Then said, "You think they'll try to pin this on me?"

Martin said, "They might."

Kessler said, to no one in particular, "For the murder of the police chief's wife."

"Yeah."

"Man," Kessler said. "It's quite a story, isn't it?"

And Martin shook his head. "Oh, yeah."

And Kessler thought, not quite there yet.

He said, "What I said earlier about Carol, that she told me she was scared of the chief, that's true, you know. She really did tell me that. And I believe she was frightened of him. Do you . . . believe that?"

Martin said, "Sure. I never liked the chief. Always thought there was something bent about him. But, then, people think I think that about all cops."

Kessler said, "Do you?"

"No," Martin said. "I do not."

Kessler said, "And yet here it is, a cop being investigated by the very cops working for him. Makes you wonder, doesn't it."

Martin said, "We should all be scared."

"That's what I was thinking," Kessler said. "I mean, if the public knew about this, they might see it in a different light, you know."

"Oh, yeah," Martin said, getting a little more interested now. "If they had seen what happened here today, these guys would have a lot to answer for."

Okay, Kessler thought, closing in. He said, "You think?"

"Fuck yes," Martin said.

"Well, maybe," Kessler said. "But the problem is, well, let's say they played this tape on the news tonight, you know what would happen. Some guy from the police department would come out and explain it and talk about the job these guys are doing, and the pressures they're under, and what actually happened here would just be forgotten. You know how that works."

"No," Martin said, "I think you're wrong about that. If they played the whole tape on the news, say, they printed the entire transcript in the *Tulsa World*, maybe even ran it on CNN, the public would smell a rat. And they'd say so."

"But," Kessler said, "I have no experience with that sort of thing."

"Don't worry," Martin said. "I do. Do you think you can get a copy of that tape made in one hour?"

Bingo.

"Well," Kessler said, "if you think it'll help."

TWENTY

Van leaned up against the chief's desk, arms folded. The chief sat in his chair, hands on his desk, gripping it, letting it go, and gripping it again. Sometimes, as he watched the television screen, his face twitched involuntarily.

The camera shot: Martin Kelly standing on the courthouse steps—not fifty yards from here—delivering a sermon from hell.

Saying now, ". . . the tape clearly indicates a detective from the Tulsa Police Department threatening to 'find something' on my client. Who is clearly innocent."

Reporter: Mr. Kelly, are you saying there's a "conspiracy"? [murmured laughter]

Martin Kelly: Now, Tanya, if I didn't know better I'd think you were trying to trick me into using that word. [laughter] You can call it a conspiracy, you can call it a square dance, you can call it whatever you want. I'm not going to tell people what they should think. The people need to make up their own minds. But I think some questions need to be asked. Like, why hasn't Mr. Clay been questioned about his wife's disappearance? Why haven't the Tulsa police checked allegations that he physically abused his wife? That she was afraid of him?

Reporter: How do you know they haven't?

Martin Kelly: Do a Freedom of Information request and ask for the police reports. I did one, and was told there aren't any. Now why is that?

Reporter: Are you saying the police department is framing

your client for the murder of Carol Macy?

Martin Kelly: I'm saying that it is awfully suspicious. Look at what's happened. My client calls the police, *he* calls *them*, and tells them about his relationship with Ms. Macy. Now, he didn't have to do that. But he did. He did it because he wanted to help. Before he made that call, they had no idea that he'd been romantically involved with her. They only know now because he voluntarily told them. So he's forthright and honest about it, and how do they respond? They accuse him of fighting with her and killing her and hiding her body. Now, would a man who did that call the police and say, hey, boys, why don't you come on down to my office so I can give you a statement? Would a man who did that want to *help* the police? Now, I'm not going to ask the citizens of this community to side with me or my client. I am only asking them to look at the facts, and ask themselves what makes sense. Use your common sense, that's all.

Reporter: But is it fair to accuse a public official of murder? Isn't that what you're doing?

Martin Kelly: Absolutely not. Mr. Clay is entitled to a presumption of innocence like anyone else, but . . . well, think of it this way: picture a guy working at McDonald's, making minimum wage, trying to feed his family. His wife disappears, just like that. Now you know in a situation like that, that fellah working at McDonald's, he's going to be a suspect in her disappearance. That's just the way it's gonna be. The police are going to want to meet with that old boy and ask him some questions. Like, how were they getting along, were they having any fights, any disputes, how was the marriage doing, and so on. And they're not just going to ask him those questions. They'll ask his friends and neighbors and family members too. Now, is that a right or decent way to treat a man who's just lost his wife? Maybe not. But the police have to check out that possibility. It's their job to do those unpleasant things that you and me don't

want to. They have to check him out *because he's her husband.*
And because he's her husband he's going to be a possible
suspect. Now, is the position of the Tulsa Police Department
going to be that the chief of police is so much more upstanding
and moral than the guy working at McDonald's that we don't
even have to look into the possibility that he may have had
something to do with his wife's disappearance? Is the position
of the Tulsa Police Department going to be: we can't ask the
chief those questions because, well, by gum, he's the chief? Is
the position of the Tulsa Police Department going to be, hey,
we've found somebody who says he had an affair with the missing woman! We've found someone to pin it on! Case closed, and
the hell with finding out the truth! Well, if that's the kind of law
enforcement you want, move back to Russia or Iran or
someplace where they don't pretend to care about freedom. In
this country, I don't think that is what people want. I think they
want and deserve law enforcement that protects the community.
Not law enforcement that protects and serves the people running City Hall. The Tulsa police are here to serve and protect
us. Not their chief. These people work for us. And I say they
must be held accountable.

Reporter: But Mr. Kelly, what was the nature of the relationship between Paul Kessler and Judge Macy?

Martin Kelly: Well, that's kinda personal. Yes, there was an
intimate relationship. It was consensual and mutual. To say any
more about it would be unfair to Ms. Macy.

Reporter: What would you say to those who say this is just a
desperate attempt to protect your client?

Martin Kelly: I would say this: my client is guilty of nothing.
Nothing. No, wait, I take that back. He is guilty. Guilty of being
naïve enough to think the Tulsa police were interested in finding
out the truth in this case. That's the problem with decent and
innocent people like Paul Kessler: they put faith in institutions

like this to protect them. Well, he was wrong to do so here. Because obviously, the Tulsa police cannot be trusted to conduct a truthful investigation in this case. Now, I'm not a politician or a judge or a public official. I'm just a man, like you. But I know what's right. I know that this country is supposed to be governed by the people for the people. I know that people died fighting for that right. They say you can't fight City Hall. Well, people, that is a lie. That is a lie perpetuated *by* City Hall. When it is the people running City Hall that are being suspected of committing the crimes, we have the right to demand that City Hall be investigated by an outside agency. That's what the Oklahoma State Bureau of Investigation [OSBI] is for. That's why we have the State Attorney General's Office. That's why we have the FBI. My client ain't afraid of the truth. Let me say that again: my client ain't afraid of the truth. So I ask City Hall to help us find the truth. Bring in investigators who will search for the truth. OSBI, FBI, attorney general. Don't matter to us who it is so long as they're looking for the truth. That's all we want. Bring in people who can investigate this crime without having to worry about losing their jobs if they get too close to the truth.

TWENTY-ONE

They watched it together at Kessler's office in the break room. Mace Mills, Kessler, Jack Feld, and Hank Patterson.

When it was done, Mace said, "Marty's been reading his Shakespeare."

"Or watching *Mr. Smith Goes to Washington*," Jack Feld said. "Probably both." He turned to Kessler. "Have they charged you with anything?"

Kessler said, "No."

"Threatened to?"

"I think so," Kessler said. "That detective that was here yesterday, he can't wait."

Jack said, "Are you scared?"

"Yeah," Kessler said. "I'm scared."

Jack said, "Is there anything I can do?"

"No."

Mace said, "That lawyer you hired, he knows how to do it. Go on the offensive, push 'em off balance."

"Yeah," Kessler said. "He's something."

"Really, Paul," Jack said. "If you need anything—"

"Thanks, Jack," Kessler said. "I'll let you know."

Jack left the room, and a few minutes later, Mace left too.

Hank Patterson remained. He just sat at the break-room table, staring impassively at Kessler.

A few moments of this went by. And Kessler thought, you can leave the room, leave him here alone. But they had known each other too long and it would be a form of betrayal.

Kessler said, "I know what I'm doing."

Hank said, "Do you?"

"Trust me," Kessler said.

Hank shook his head. "I know you better than your lawyer does," he said. "This conspiracy bullshit, it ain't you. Martin wouldn't have taken to those courthouse steps unless you wanted him to."

Kessler shrugged. "It's not a bad strategy," he said.

Hank said, "Whose idea was it?"

"His."

"You sure about that?"

"Well," Kessler said, "I may have encouraged him a little."

"Bobbie told me you called the house Wednesday night," Hank said. "Like you needed a favor or something. I called back and you weren't home. I called your cell and you didn't answer." He said, "Do you want to tell me what happened now?"

Kessler said, "No."

"Why not?"

"Because it's not your place to know."

Necessary as it was, it felt awful to say it. They hadn't served in any war together or saved each other's lives. But they had worked together for six years and were close friends. Kessler was godfather to Hank's daughter, and if he ever found a woman he wanted willing to marry him, there was no doubt that Hank would stand as best man.

"You thought it was my place Wednesday night," Hank said. "Now you say it isn't?"

"Hank," Kessler said, "just stay out of it. Please."

"Is it because I used to be a cop?"

"Oh, shit," Kessler said. "No. That's not it."

"What then?"

"Hank," Kessler said, "you've got a wife, children. If things go right, I'll get out of this mess. If they don't, I am going to jail. That's it. If it comes to that, I'm not going to watch you get five years for being an accomplice."

"An accomplice to what?" Hank said. "I know you didn't kill that woman. Tell me what it is you're worried about."

"Goddammit, Hank," Kessler said. "You're not listening to me."

It didn't faze him much. He continued to sit there quietly, letting the tension dissipate. Then said, "Come on, Paul. It's just us. This secrecy stuff, that's . . . that's for other people."

The second hand on the clock wall clicked by and there was only the sound of the refrigerator's buzz and Kessler looked uneasily to the open door. Then he walked and closed it and turned to the man.

"You're right," he said. "I didn't kill her. Not even accidentally. Although I suspect if I hadn't slept with her, she'd be alive now. What I told the cops, that's mostly the truth. What I didn't tell them is—I know she's dead."

Hank leaned forward in his seat.

"That's right," Kessler said. "I know."

After a while, Hank said, "How would you—" Then stopped himself and held his hand up to stop Kessler from saying anything.

Hank said, "Hypothetically speaking, if you found a woman's dead body in your home and thought that woman's body was put there in order to frame you, would you call the police?"

Kessler said, "Not if I thought the police put her there."

"In your house?"

Kessler shook his head.

"My car."

Hank leaned back in his chair. He said, "Jesus Christ."

Kessler said, "Hypothetically speaking."

Twenty-Two

Mayor Rhonda Brett said, "Sam, you understand that you don't have to prove anything to me." She said, "You understand that, don't you?"

Chief Clay said, "I understand what you mean."

The mayor said, "We've known each other for . . . when did I bring you on here?"

They were in her office, on the top floor of City Hall. Mayor Rhonda Brett, the Margaret Thatcher of the Southwest. Sans the English accent and knowledge of Balkan strife, but just as shrewd and every bit as tough. While she hadn't stood toe to toe with Reagan and Gorbachev, she'd managed to remain in executive office nine years, two years longer than Dame Maggie, and had attended any number of Neighborhood Club meetings where people came mostly just to try to roust her and ended up getting a hell of a lot more than they bargained for when she systematically belittled them instead. Toughest mayor the city'd had in twenty years, and didn't she just know it too? Reminding Sam Clay now that she hired him and she could fire him.

The chief said, "It was five years ago."

The mayor said, "I had no doubt then about your capabilities for this job. And I have no doubt about them now."

Chief Clay said, "I'm glad to hear that, ma'am."

"But, Sam," she said, "it's a political job. Isn't it?"

Chief Clay shifted in his chair. "Yeah . . ."

"That's something people don't understand about public service," she said. "About people like you and me. People in positions of leadership. We take on huge responsibilities, huge burdens. They can't understand the burdens we have. Not just the work, but the perceptions too. Do you understand what I'm talking about?"

Chief Clay said, "I do."

"My daughters," the mayor said, "they don't understand why anyone with any sense would go into public service. They think it's too brutal. I suppose they're right. But they don't know that we, we act out of duty."

Chief Clay said, "Absolutely."

"And part of that duty," the Mayor said, "is to maintain public perception. Isn't it."

Chief Clay said, "I'm not sure what you mean."

"Oh, Sam," the Mayor said, "you know exactly what I mean."

Chief Clay recoiled and tried to hide it. That she would speak to him like this . . . like he was a child. A child being called into the principal's office. He said, "If you're talking about what that lawyer said at the press conference this morning—"

"Sam," the mayor said, "before you say anything, I want to tell you something. Listen very closely to me: I do not for a minute believe a word of what that lawyer said at that press conference. I do not believe a word of what he said. Okay?"

"Well," the chief said, "I appreciate that."

The mayor made a dismissive gesture. Then she said, "But what I think doesn't really matter, does it?"

"Excuse me?"

The mayor said, "It's the perception that matters. The public perception. That's not fair, but it's the reality of politics." She said, "That's something people like you and I understand, isn't it."

"Ma'am," Chief Clay said, "are you . . . asking me for my resignation?"

"Resignation?" the mayor said. "Of course not. I don't want you to resign. Why would you think that?"

"I don't know," Chief Clay said. "I must have misunderstood. You were talking about perception."

"Yes," the mayor said, "but not because I want you to resign. I want you to stay."

Chief Clay relaxed, a little.

"But," the mayor said, "I am requesting the OSBI investigate Carol's disappearance."

The chief said, "What?"

"I'm requesting the OSBI take over the investigation into Carol's disappearance," the mayor said. "Effective today."

The chief sat up in his chair. "May I ask why?"

"I think that's the best way to handle it," the mayor said. "I've discussed it with the city attorney and he agrees. Sam, it's about perception. There cannot be any appearance of impropriety on this. It makes the city vulnerable to criticism."

"The city, huh?"

"Yeah, Sam," the mayor said, her voice firm. "The city. What were you thinking?"

Chief Clay said, "I was thinking about your campaign for reelection coming up in the fall. Is it possible you're concerned about being vulnerable yourself?"

The mayor held his gaze. She said, "Sam, I'm doing you a favor. You're an employee at will, serving this city at my discretion. If I thought you had anything to do with Carol's disappearance, I'd fire you right now. Ponder that before you accuse me of selling you out." She said, "That's all."

And like that, he was dismissed.

Twenty-Three

Jamie Flatt told her son to put the puppy in the back seat of the car because she was getting on the gear shift and interfering with Mama's driving.

Tucker Flatt said, "But she likes it up here."

"In the back, Tucker," Jamie said. "Molly's supposed to ride in the back."

Molly was a three-month-old puppy they'd picked up from the SPCA a few weeks ago. They hadn't told Jamie what breed Molly was, but the little scamp had developed paws the size of bran muffins and Jamie began to see signs of a German shepherd/Labrador mix that was sure to grow to seventy pounds. Count on spending thirty dollars a month for dog food, she thought.

Tucker put Molly in the back seat.

Well, he really was very sweet with the puppy. He'd promised to feed her and take care of her and housebreak her. Hell, Jamie thought, he might even do it.

He was a good kid, Tucker Flatt. Bratty like any other kid at times, but a good kid with a good heart. Eight years old, blonde-haired with the tall-bodied good looks of his father, though showing no signs of his father's essential meanness.

Tucker said, "Mama?"

Jamie said, "Yes, honey."

"How long am I gonna stay at Grandma's?"

"Just a couple of days, baby."

"Are you going someplace?" the boy said. "Or are you just working?"

Jamie hesitated. "Well, honey, I'm not really going away or working. I have to take care of some things."

"What kind of things?"

"Grown-up things, baby."

Tucker said, "Mama?"

"Yes, honey."

"Is it true you work in a bar?"

"Who told you that, honey?" Jamie said. "Somebody at school?"

"Yes."

"Yeah, honey. It's true."

"What do you do there?"

"I serve grown-ups things to drink," Jamie said. "It's honest work, honey."

"They have girls there, too?"

"Never mind that, baby."

Tucker was silent then. And Jamie turned to him and brushed his hair back with her free hand.

"The kids at school," she said, "do they say other things too?"

"Yes, ma'am."

"Mean things?"

"Sometimes."

"Well, Tucker," Jamie said. "Kids sometimes say things that aren't nice. You just have to learn to ignore them. Best thing to do is stay away from them."

Tucker said, "What if they don't stay away from you?"

Jamie said, "Well then, you tell 'em they need to stop."

"And if they don't stop?"

"If they don't stop, Tucker, you might have to fight 'em back."

Jamie's mother's house was in Claremore. Jamie pulled her

Pontiac Grand Prix into the driveway and got Tucker's bag out of the trunk and the pup out of the back seat. She handed Molly's leash to Tucker and crouched down to speak to him.

"Son," she said, "when I said you may have to fight back, I only meant that you should fight if you've got no other choice. Understand? You are a good boy and if you do right you're going to grow up to be a good man. I know you will. But I don't ever want you starting fights. You're too big for that. Do you understand me?"

"Yeah."

"Excuse me?"

"Yes, ma'am."

Jamie said, "You know what a bully is, don't you?"

"Yes, ma'am."

"It's the worst thing you can be, Tuck. The worst thing you can be. You become a bully and you'll bring more shame on your mama than she'll ever get working at a girlie bar. Okay?"

"Okay, Mama."

She kissed him and hugged him and said, "You be good to Grandma now."

Hank came into his office and said, "I think I've got one."

Kessler said, "Yeah?"

"A 'seventy-one model," Hank said. "It's not a 3.0 model though. It's a 2.8. But they look identical."

Kessler said, "What color is it?"

"It's a metallic blue," Hank said. "Not really light blue. But I think it'll pass."

"Let's hope so," Kessler said. "It's not like they're going to have a picture of the original. Where is it?"

"Laguna Beach, California."

"Oh, shit," Kessler said. "How soon can they deliver it?"

"They can get it delivered here in three days."

"I don't like that," Kessler said. "That's not going to be soon enough."

"But," Hank said, "they've got another set of cars they're delivering tomorrow. That truck leaves tonight for West Palm Beach, Florida. It can make a stop in Dallas."

"Dallas?"

"I can meet them there," Hank said. "Drive it back here in five hours."

Kessler said, "*I* can meet them there."

"That's the worst thing you can do," Hank said. "You'd be followed or seen or caught somehow. You need help, man. I told you that before."

"Hank—"

"I've got the guy on hold," Hank said. "You want the car or not?"

Jeanne came to the door.

"Excuse me," she said, "Paul?"

"What is it, Jeanne?"

"There's a Jamie Flatt here to see you."

"Who is she?"

"She doesn't have an appointment," Jeanne said. "She said she wants to talk to you about Sam Clay?"

Hank was still looking at him. He held a hand up to say, make a decision.

Kessler said, "Okay," and Hank walked out.

Jeanne watched Hank go by. She said, "Okay, you'll see her?"

"Yeah, I'll see her."

She was an attractive woman, whoever she was. Tall, long-legged, and shapely, if you liked them that way. The kind of girl you remember from high school that you never had a chance with because she dug the tough, dangerous guys who worked construction after school and always had good pot and, though the same age as you, seemed like they were about ten years older. Back then, girls like that had been unattainable and unapproachable. They seemed older too, yet, strangely, they too were the same age. They lived for the day, and those years from age fourteen to eighteen were their days. They owned them. They seemed to know things about life, sex and drugs that you still hoped to learn, and though you may have had college and careers and money to look forward to, you would still feel eternally grateful if one of these teenage goddesses called you by your first name in the school hall. Some of those girls got fat, burned-up, and washed-up by the age of twenty-one. And some still remained hot-looking as they aged.

Jamie Flatt was one of them that remained hot-looking.

She looked like she was about thirty, though not trying to hold on to anything. Sitting in the conference room, she wore a serious expression, but she had the look of a woman who liked to laugh.

Kessler said, "What did you want to talk to me about?"

Jamie said, "I work at Cassy's, do you know it?"

"Yeah," Kessler said, "I know where it is."

"I've worked there for about a year and a half," she said. "I'm not a dancer, okay? I'm a waitress."

"Okay."

Jamie said, "I came here to talk to you about Sam Clay."

"Chief Clay?"

"That's the one."

Kessler remembered Carol telling him that she thought Sam was seeing another woman. Be careful, he thought. He said, "Is he a friend of yours?"

"You mean am I sleeping with him?" the woman said. "God, no. I had dinner with him a couple of times, but . . . no. There was nothing like that."

"How do you know him?"

"He comes by the club sometimes," she said. "He—"

"Stop right there," Kessler said. "Chief Clay goes to Cassy's?"

"Sure," Jamie said. "Well, not really during regular hours. Just on special occasions."

Kessler looked at the woman. Good-looking, tough . . . but what was her game? He said, "Would you mind if I taped this conversation?"

"Yeah, I would mind," she said. "I came here in confidence, you know."

"I know that," Kessler said. "But . . . well, never mind. You were saying that the chief used to come to Cassy's."

"Yeah."

"For what?"

"Like I said, special occasions." Jamie said, "For the cops. He only came to a couple."

"Special, what, parties for the cops?"

"Yeah," she said. "Like for a cop's birthday. Promotions. Bachelor parties, things like that."

"They'd have parties at a strip club?"

"Sure," she said. "Van would set 'em up."

"Who's Van?"

"Greg," she said. "Vannerson. Everybody calls him Van. He's a lieutenant with the Tulsa police. He was the one who'd set the parties up."

"Do you mean parties with . . . you and the other girls?"

"No," Jamie said. "Not with *me* and the other girls. With the other girls. I don't do that."

Kessler said, "You don't do what?"

"Fuck for money."

Kessler must have made some sort of face or coughing noise because the woman said, "Sorry." To excuse her language, apparently.

Kessler said, "I wasn't implying that you, well, you know."

The woman shrugged. "It doesn't matter," she said. "Yes, the girls fu—have sex for money at Cassy's. It's not that big a secret."

"It's not?"

Jamie said, "Do you go there?"

"To Cassy's?"

"Yeah."

Kessler said, "It's been a couple of years."

"Yeah," she said. "I've never seen you there. Not for you?"

"Girls, you mean?"

"Well—"

"I like girls," Kessler said.

"Well, that's," Jamie said, "kinda obvious."

Until then, it hadn't occurred to him that she would know about the affair with Carol. But then, after Martin's press conference, the whole town knew. This woman sitting across from him knew—a total stranger. It wasn't fair to Carol, and he didn't much like it either. But it was done. Still, the fact that it was his doing didn't stop him from resenting this woman for making a casual reference to it.

Kessler said, "To tell you the truth, I've never been a big fan of those places. It's demeaning."

"Demeaning?" Jamie said, "To who?"

"To everyone," Kessler said. "I love women . . . But that sort of environment . . . well, you might as well have a bunch of guys pass a *Playboy* magazine around a circle."

"Maybe you oughtta teach Sunday school."

"All right then," Kessler said. "I'm a hypocrite. But I . . . listen, I don't want to argue with you. Okay?"

"Okay."

"You were talking about this Lieutenant Van."

"Vannerson."

"Lieutenant Vannerson," Kessler said. "He used to set these parties up?"

"Yes."

"With cops and prostitutes?"

"Yes."

Kessler said, "I don't believe it."

The woman seemed to smile. She said, "Does it shock you?"

"Yes," Kessler said. "It shocks me."

"You think it's immoral?"

"Prostitution?"

"Yeah."

Kessler remembered defending a postal worker who got caught soliciting a prostitute on Eleventh Street. He cut a plea for the guy and got him a six-month suspended sentence. Then went home and told a girlfriend about it who was visiting from Germany. He told her about the arrest and the plea and the poor guy's wife sitting in the courtroom while he confessed the solicitation to the judge. The German woman said, more than once, "But what did he do wrong?" Until Kessler finally understood the cultural difference behind the confusion and said, "Prostitution's illegal here." And she said, "It ees?" with honest surprise.

Now he said, "I don't know if it's immoral or not. But it is against the law. I mean, cops?"

Jamie said, "Man, where have you been?"

"What?"

"Cops and whores?" Jamie said. "I guess you don't know either very well. Pardon my French, but do you know how many cops are getting head in their squad cars from prostitutes? And I mean, like, regularly."

"No, I don't."

"It's plenty, trust me."

Kessler said, "Was Sam Clay having sex with prostitutes?"

"Oh, yeah."

"More than once?"

"Sure."

Kessler said, "Is that what you came here to tell me?"

"Partly," she said. "But I have my own reasons too. Selfish reasons."

"What do you mean?"

"I'm afraid of Sam," she said. "I think he may hurt me. Kill me even."

"Why would he do that?" Kessler said. "Is there something you know?"

"Something I know? I don't think the things I know have anything to do with it," Jamie said. "He's got a thing for me, that's all."

Kessler said, "Did you have a relationship with him?"

"I told you I didn't."

"Not even once?"

"No. Not even once."

"Why not?"

"My God, have you ever met the man?" Jamie said. "He's a drip."

"He's not a ladies' man?"

"Not even close," she said. "He knows nothing, *nothing,* about women. I mean, what kind of idiot asks a woman out on a date just after he gets done screwing a prostitute?"

"I think plenty of men do that."

"Not when the woman sees him go in the back room with the prostitute and then come back out fifteen minutes later."

"Oh."

Jamie said, "The guy's just creepy. He's obviously got issues with women. He doesn't seem to see a problem with doing what he did."

"Did you know he was doing that before you had dinner with him?"

"No," Jamie said, "I didn't know. But I should have. I misunderstood him at first. He seemed so clean-cut, you know. He had manners and he dressed well. I thought . . . well, we don't get many decent men in a place like that."

"I understand," Kessler said. "What changed your mind?"

"We went out once and he more or less behaved himself," Jamie said. "He took me to dinner at Freddie's Steakhouse in Sapulpa. And he was nice. He talked about his work. He poured the wine, opened the car door. And at the end of the night, he shook my hand. I didn't much like him. He just seemed like a nerd. But creepy, you know. Anyway, he asked me out again and I went. I don't know why; I think I may have felt sorry for him. And when we went out that second time, that's when he got all psycho on me."

"What happened?"

"Well, he didn't do anything real bad," Jamie said. "We went to dinner, and he talked about how lonely he was, and how his wife didn't understand him, and shit I've heard dozens of times. And it was just sorta depressing. Then after dinner he drove straight to a hotel. Well, this was news to me. Usually, a man wants to get you in bed, they'll drop little hints at dinner. A dirty joke maybe, some sexual comment. And if the woman responds, you know, favorably, they go to somebody's place or maybe a hotel. Signs, signals. You work up to it, right? Well, when we had dinner, that second time, there was practically none of that. It was just depressing and lonely. So when he drove to this hotel, I was, like, what gave you this idea? I really think the guy was inexperienced. So I said, you know, trying to be nice, 'Sam, no. This is not what I want.' And he went apeshit. Called me a bitch, a tease. Said, 'What the fuck is your problem?' Well, when a man talks like that to you, you know it's

161

just one step away from him giving you a black eye. So I said, you take me home right now. And he kept bitching but he drove me home."

"And that was all?"

"That's all that happened that night," she said. "He asked me out a couple more times, and I always said no. And then, last Tuesday, after work, I saw him in the parking lot at Cassy's. He was there waiting for me. He asked me why I hadn't called him. And he told me it wasn't nice to avoid him. He told me, 'You need to call me.' And he was touching me then. He put his nasty finger on my stomach. Which was exposed because I was wearing one of those short shirts."

"That's all?"

"What do you mean, 'that's all?' " Jamie said, "Can't you see that that scared me?"

"It did?"

"Yes, it scared me." She said, "Enough that I told Van about it the next day."

"The next day? You mean Wednesday?"

She nodded.

"What time did you tell Van?"

"What time?" she said. "I don't know. Maybe sometime after eight o'clock."

"Van was at the club that night?"

"Sure."

"What did Lieutenant Van say he'd do?"

Jamie said, "He said he'd talk to him."

Kessler said, "So the chief of police accosts you in a parking lot and you ask a lieutenant to talk to him about it?"

The woman said, "You don't know Van."

Kessler said, "What is he, some sort of godfather?"

"No," she said. "I mean, well, yeah, sort of. He's got a lot of influence in the department. He's not a captain, but his officers swear by him. They give him total loyalty. But he's not a gangster or anything like that. He's actually a pretty good guy."

"Who runs a prostitution ring."

"Maybe," she said. "But it's for his men. I don't think he does it for money. Besides, he's not doing anything different than a lot of people."

"How do you mean?"

"People use sex to sell everything," she said. "And not just on television. You see that movie *Striptease* with Demi Moore?"

"I think so."

The woman was smiling at him. "You think so, uh. Well, what'd you pay to see that? Six bucks?"

"I suppose."

Jamie said, "And what was it you were paying that money to see?"

Kessler smiled now. "I don't think that's the same thing."

"It's not much different," Jamie said. "Not much. I used to work as a secretary for a pharmaceutical company. You know how they sell their drugs? They hire women, usually with college degrees, but always, always, babes. You never saw some fat chick selling their products. And these women set up wine and cheese parties for doctors and they dress up and they smile and they tell these doctors how smart they are and what wonderful work they're doing. For what? So the doctors will buy the company's drugs. Now I ask you, what is *that* all about? Maybe they're not lying down with the doctors, but they're selling themselves all the same."

Kessler said, "I think you're casting the net a little wide."

"Maybe," she said. "Maybe the girls at Cassy's go a little farther. But not much farther. It's the same ballpark. Anyway, at least the girls at Cassy's aren't pushing drugs."

Kessler found himself studying this woman. If he'd met her under different circumstances, he might ask her to have a drink.

She was attractive to be sure. But she might also be one of those women you could spend a few hours with at a bar just talking philosophy. With a few laughs mixed in.

He said, "You don't have to justify anything to me."

"I'm not trying to," she said, a little edge in her voice. "I'm a waitress. But some of those girls are all right. Some of them are my friends."

"Okay," Kessler said. "You said Sam Clay scared you?"

"I only told you about the first time," she said. "There was a second time. Last night. Last night, he came to my apartment. My home, where I live with my son."

"You have a son?"

"Yes. He's eight years old. He's a good boy."

"Where's his father?"

"He Hank Snowed on us."

"He what?"

"He left us," she said. "Two years ago. Just left. No explanation."

"I'm sorry."

The woman shrugged. "I don't miss him," she said. "He was abusive. Anyway . . . Sam. Sam came over to my apartment and he grabbed me again. This time it was worse. He grabbed me and tried to kiss me and tried to pull my clothes off. I finally had to rack him, but I didn't connect as well as I hoped. He grabbed me . . . he grabbed me by the neck and threw me down. Luckily, I landed on the couch. So I just screamed and screamed."

"And?"

"That more or less took care of it," she said. "Soon someone started banging on the door and he opened it and he left, shoved my neighbor as he walked out."

Kessler said, "This was last night?"

"Yeah."

"Did you call the police?"

Jamie said, "Well, what do you think?"

"I think you should have called the police."

"Really," she said. "Didn't you accuse them of conspiring to frame you?"

"Yeah, but—"

"Yeah, but," she said, "I've got a lot to lose. I more or less work in a whorehouse and I've got a son that can be taken away from me. I know how those guys work. I think, better than you do."

Kessler said, "Don't be so sure."

"Well," Jamie said, "when he grabbed me by the neck, I knew, I just knew then that he'd killed his wife."

Kessler leaned forward. "How do you know?"

"I don't *know* know," she said. "I just know. He's crazy. And he's getting crazier."

Kessler said, "How do you know I didn't do it?"

"Because I know he did," she said. "I know about him from personal experience. And I know about what you had going with his wife from what I read in the paper. I think he found out about it and he killed her. It's really that simple, isn't it?"

"*I* think so," Kessler said. "Why did you come to see me?"

"I thought I could help you," she said. "And I hoped you could help me."

"You can help me," Kessler said. "If you want to. I don't know what I could do for you."

Jamie said, "You can help put Sam Clay in jail."

"I'm not a policeman."

"But he is," she said. "That's the point. I can't go to the police for help. You might go to jail for murder. I might lose my son."

"What about this lieutenant friend of yours?" Kessler said. "Why not go to him?"

"Van?" she said. "I went to him before, and it didn't do any good."

"Have you talked to Van since Wednesday?"

"No."

"Seen him since then?"

"No, actually."

"Do you think he talked to Clay for you?"

"He said he would."

"Yeah, but did he?"

"I think he did."

Kessler said, "Do you think he went to the chief's house that night?"

"I don't know where he went after we talked," Jamie said. "But he did leave about an hour after we talked."

Kessler said, "But if the chief was home, and Carol was there . . . ," thinking out loud. He stopped and looked at the woman. Yes, a good-looking woman sitting there in her short black skirt and clingy brown sweater like she was waiting for Mike Hammer to return from a bridge he'd just thrown a guy off, intriguing him more and more. Looking very good indeed. But then, that was his weakness, wasn't it?

He said, "I don't know."

Jamie said, "What do you mean?"

"I mean," he said, "I don't know about you. I've had some very strange things happen to me in the last few days. How do I know about you? How do I know you weren't sent here to set me up?"

Jamie said, "How would I set you up?"

"I don't know."

"I just told you the chief of police knocked me around. That I think he killed his wife. That a police lieutenant is a pimp," she said. "Would I tell you those things if I were trying to set you up?"

"Actually," Kessler said, "you might. Say I believed everything you told me and tried to use it in my defense and the whole thing turns out to be completely false. I'd be discredited and that much more suspect. If that happened, it would be that much easier for the people who want to see me hang."

Jamie said, "So you don't trust me."

"Lady," Kessler said, "I don't *know* you. Are *you* taping this conversation?"

"What?"

"You heard me," Kessler said. "Are you taping this conversation?"

Jamie stood up and put her purse on the conference room table. She turned the purse upside down and emptied out its contents. Then she half threw, half slid the purse over to him. She remained standing.

"Check it if you like," she said. "Do you want me to get undressed too? So you can see if I'm wearing a wire?"

Kessler looked at her for a long time.

Then he said, "No."

"I can take a polygraph if you want."

Kessler said, "It isn't necessary. Sit down. Please."

"I told you before," she said, "I don't—"

"I know," Kessler said. "You don't."

TWENTY-FOUR

There was a man inside the motel room holding his wife and her mother hostage with a shotgun. The call had come out over the radio as shots fired and by the time the first patrol officers arrived, the man had already killed the father-in-law. Now he was telling the police negotiator that he wanted them to bring his ten-year-old daughter to the motel just so he could talk to her, which meant he wanted to hug her and kiss her and tell her he loved her before killing her, Mommy, Grandma, and then himself. It was a request they couldn't possibly comply with and they hadn't yet been able to trick the man into moving in front of the window so the tactical team could get a clean shot at him.

There were about thirty cops there, fifteen or so in SWAT gear. Lieutenant Van and Buddy Matlock stood a safe distance away, behind a police truck.

Van said, "I think the guy's gone nuts."

"It's an old story," Buddy said. "She filed a protective order against him and that set him off."

"No," Van said, "not this turd. I'm talking about the chief."

"Oh," Buddy said. "What happened?"

"Don't you know?" Van said. "No. I suppose you don't. The mayor told him this morning that she's calling in OSBI."

"Really?" Buddy said. "How did you find out?"

Van said, "He told me. The chief. He was practically crying when he told me. Man, everyone will know by tomorrow."

Buddy said, "Well, that sucks."

There was some shouting in the background. Someone yelling through a bullhorn. "If she dies, you die! You hear me! If she dies, you die!" The guy shouting something back.

"It's that fucking lawyer," Van said. "He called in the lead detective, Gilvetti, and he played him. He's playing us."

"Who are you talking about?"

"You know," Van said. "The lawyer."

"Oh, him."

"Yeah, him." Van said, "The lawyer pushed Gil's buttons and got him so mad he pretty much admitted he wanted to frame his ass. Then he got his own lawyer to go on television and ask for an outside investigator." Van said, "Smart fucker."

"He got lucky."

"Better to be lucky than good," Van said. "He may have got lucky with Ray. But that thing with Gil, man, that was a smart fuckin' play."

Buddy looked at Van uncertainly.

"Van . . . ?"

"What?"

"You're talking as if you almost admire the guy."

"Well you gotta admit, for a lawyer, he's pretty smart. It's almost like he's got a little cop in him."

The thing was, Van thought, the man wouldn't run. He may have run from Ray, but he wouldn't run from them. If only he had run and hid, it would have made things easier. But instead of moving away from those who would hunt him, he moved toward them. Like calling the police before they called him. That had been smart. That had given him an advantage. Instead of allowing the police to find out about his fling with the judge, he had told the police first. And in doing so, he had deprived the police from using incriminating evidence against him. Things like: *we have witnesses who saw you have dinner with Carol*

Macy. We found strands of her hair in your house. They were all meaningless now. Because the man had been up-front about his relationship with the woman. Now all he had to say was: *of course you found her hair in my house. I told you I was fucking her.* A goddamn lawyer's trick. Where the lawyer tells the jury all the weaknesses of his case before the opponent does and takes that juicy hambone right off the other guy's plate.

But in this arena, it meant more than that. This qualified as a first strike. It was an offensive measure because the man had taken the finger of suspicion off himself and pointed it straight at Sam Clay. It was like they had planned to see him forty yards up the trail and shoot him in the back, and he suddenly stepped out of the woods five feet in front and rushed them. They hadn't been ready for it.

"Van," Buddy said, "what is *with* you? You think this is some sort of game?"

"It is a game," Van said. "But he hasn't figured everything out. He knows he's been set up. But he doesn't know who did it. He knows we took his gun. But he doesn't know we took the tire iron out of his car."

"Hey," Buddy said. "That's right."

Buddy had been so uptight, he'd almost forgotten about that little trump card. But then, Van thought, Ray had been the one who'd taken the tire iron out of the man's BMW and smacked it into the dead woman's skull. Not Buddy. Now, it had her blood on it and maybe even a little bit of her hair. Even if they gave it back to the poor guy, he wouldn't be able to wash off that sort of DNA. Modern police procedures, using chemical tests, could trace her spoor easily. Let the lawyer feel confident for now. When they helped the investigators discover the tire iron, with its BMW insignia, he would know that he hadn't been dealing with a bunch of clowns.

"OSBI," Buddy said, shaking his head. "Makes me nervous too."

"It's Sam Clay they're investigating," Van said. "At least for now. But they'll be coming back to the lawyer soon enough."

But there was a real possibility an OSBI investigation could spill over to him, Van thought. Oh, yeah. It could spill over to him with a fucking vengeance. That was why he'd gotten involved in this mess in the first place. He'd walked into the chief's house and seen Judge Macy dead on the floor. After the initial surprise, he'd been foolish enough to think he was lucky. Had he not walked in when he did, who knows what the chief might have done? He might have called the deputy chief or the district attorney or Captain Devereaux. And then what would have happened? Questions and then answers. And then more questions and more answers. *Just tell us what happened, chief. Cop to cop, just tell us what happened. You had an argument? What was it about? She accused you of what? Sleeping with prostitutes? At Cassy's? Hmmm. Yeah, we've heard about what goes on there. Tell us some more. Yeah, that Lieutenant Van treats his patrol officers right, doesn't he?*

Sayyy, wasn't it Van who transported that drug informant to Missouri a few weeks ago? We always did think it strange that he and the other two officers all three just happened to leave the car when the informant was whacked. Maybe we need to give further consideration to all of that.

Maybe it wouldn't have happened that way. But you couldn't be sure. Especially with someone of Sam Clay's constitution. The man was weak. Sam Clay came from Houston and someone had once told Van that he'd only spent two years on the street and spent the next twenty-five in administration. He'd never once drawn his service weapon, they said. It showed. Sam wasn't strong enough to play, strong enough to bluff it out.

So, Van surveyed the dead wife on the floor and Sam blubbering like a baby and thought, why leave the door open? And the added bonus to bailing the chief out was to have the chief under his complete control. It seemed like a good plan at the time.

But then Ray had fucked up, and the lawyer got away. Thank God he'd taken the tire iron away from Ray. If he'd left it with him, it would have been found at the scene in Ray's patrol car after he was killed . . . how would they have explained that?

And now Sam Clay was falling apart. Jesus, the OSBI. It was only a matter of time—a day maybe, two at most—before Sam got a lawyer and then they'd probably all be fucked. Maybe Sam would be cool with his lawyer and stick with the story, but odds weren't comforting on that. It was just as likely he'd tell the lawyer what happened and say, "It was an accident, I swear, it was an accident," and his lawyer and the DA might start laying the groundwork for an involuntary manslaughter plea agreement, seven to ten years, suspended sentence if Sam resigns from the department, takes some anger management courses and . . .

. . . and agrees to tell us some more about what's going on at Cassy's. Agrees to tell us what he knows about Greg Vannerson.

Who would like to take it in that direction? Apart from the OSBI, there would be one major league asshole captain of the detectives who went by the name of Mal Devereaux. Oh, yeah, he could see that choirboy licking his lips over this one. Devereaux had been looking for a way to sink him for years. Devereaux with his goddamn Barney Fife picture on his desk, trying to be cute. What did Mal Devereaux know about patrol? About the street? About the men out there in the cold and the shit? What did he know about the working officer, busting his ass to pay child support while he sat in a warm office and drew a captain's pay? What did he know about these men? How could he know? Who was he to judge?

Buddy said, "Do you want me to put it in his house?" Meaning, the tire iron.

Shit, Van thought, he wasn't going to entrust that job to Buddy. Not after what had happened to Ray.

"No," Van said. "I'll take care of it."

Three shots rang out in succession.

The lieutenant and the patrol officer hunched their shoulders, then heard another cop yell out: "I got him! Goddammit, I got him!"

The lieutenant and the patrol officer relaxed and found themselves smiling in spite of all their troubles.

"Two lives saved," Van said. "And tomorrow some asshole in the paper will write about how the bloodthirsty pigs cut the turd down in the prime of his life."

"With a lawsuit to follow," Buddy said. "But that's the job."

TWENTY-FIVE

Jamie repeated the story about Sam Clay assaulting her and Greg Vannerson's parties while Kessler typed it into his computer. There were starts and stops with Kessler asking her to hold up while he finished sentences. It would have gone faster if Jeanne was there to type it, but she had gone home for the night and he needed to get this down as soon as possible. They finished putting together the affidavit after about an hour and a half, and Kessler printed it out and had her sign it.

Kessler said, "I need you to come back tomorrow so Jeanne can notarize your signature. Can you do that?"

Jamie said, "Yeah, I can do that. Can you give me a copy of it then?"

"Sure. But I don't want you to show it to anyone for a few days. Okay?"

"Okay," she said, though she seemed unsure.

Kessler said, "Just trust me."

"Trust you?" she said, a little smile forming in her eyes. "Buddy, I don't know you."

Kessler smiled at the callback. "No, you don't know me," he said. Then he looked at her and she looked back at him and he saw the green in her eyes and heard himself say, "Maybe when this whole thing is over . . ."

"What?"

Kessler said, "Never mind."

Jamie said, "You and me on . . . a date? That'd be kind of

freaky, wouldn't it?"

"Forget it."

"You don't waste any time, do you?"

"I'm sorry. Forget it."

She studied him for a few moments. "I don't know," she said, affecting a serious tone. "You'd have to do something about those sideburns."

"These?"

"Yeah, those would have to go," she said. "Look like little mice."

"Next you'll be picking out my clothes," Kessler said. He stood up. "I'll walk you to your car."

They were the last ones out of the building. Kessler turned on the alarm and locked up. It was late and the night was cool.

At her car, she turned and asked him, "Did you love her?"

Kessler said, "Excuse me?"

"Oh, come on," she said. "I can ask that, can't I?"

Kessler looked at her and supposed she could. He hadn't discussed it truthfully with anybody. He'd intentionally given the detectives the impression that he was a cold, passionless prick who'd used Carol Macy. And maybe that was partially accurate. But he'd felt something more for Carol than lust, though he doubted it was love. But he couldn't let the detectives know that. They would have exploited it and made it something more than it was, made it fit into their theory of their case against him. It would be easier for them to believe he didn't murder the woman if he said he felt no love for her. The man in love was much more suspicious. The man who declares his love for the woman is more likely to violate the protective order, more likely to plot her misery, more likely to end her life. Ironic perhaps, but there it was.

"No," he said. "I guess I didn't. We had some good times, for a while. Then I think we found out we probably didn't like each other very much. I suppose there was never really any future in it."

Jamie said, "Maybe that's how she wanted it."

"Maybe," Kessler said. "She never said what she wanted."

"That bother you?"

"What does it matter?" Kessler said. He looked at the woman. "Did she love her husband?"

"He wouldn't have known it if she did," Jamie said. "I can say that because I know him. He seemed pretty miserable. But, no, I really don't know what they felt for each other. Aren't all marriages mysteries?"

"Perhaps," Kessler said. ". . . She was a good judge."

"What?"

"She really was," he said. "She was fair, open-minded, conscientious. And very smart. She liked the law, respected it. Not every judge is like that, you know."

Jamie looked at him curiously and realized he was serious. "You are a very strange man," she said. "I'll see you in the morning."

Kessler said, "Wait a minute."

"What?"

"You're not going back to your house, are you?"

"Well . . ."

"You can't go back there. What about Sam?"

"What do you want me to do—move?"

"Why don't you stay at a hotel for a few days?" Kessler said, "Until this thing settles down."

"This thing may never settle down," Jamie said. "And hotels cost money."

"I'll pay for it," Kessler said. He smiled. "The hotel, I mean."

She wagged a finger at him.

"Come on," he said. "At least for tonight." He took five

twenty-dollar bills from his wallet and held them toward her. "Please."

Jamie said, "A witness fee?"

"Yeah," he said. "A witness fee."

She hesitated, then took the money. "I'll pay it back," she said.

"If you like," Kessler said. "But you don't have to."

She said, "I'll be at the Motel 6. On South Harvard."

Kessler looked at her curiously, and she said, "That's in case you need to call me, studley. That's all."

Kessler drove home and fixed himself a drink. He loosened his tie and sat down to the piano. He played few a strains of "My Funny Valentine." Then "I Have Dreamed," and "I've Grown Accustomed to Her Face." Then made a few attempts at something called "Dear Heart," which didn't really work. But it succeeded in taking his mind off Carol Macy for a while.

His mother had made him take piano lessons when he was a boy, and he found out quickly that he liked it. It had been difficult to admit that at that age. Curiously, his love of the piano led him to join the wrestling team in junior high. His dad had looked him in the eye and said, "Paul, in this life, a man who plays the piano has to learn how to defend himself." It was the sort of half serious/half inane observation his father liked to make. Paul picked up the habit himself, and by the time he was in high school and had become proficient at throwing other boys on the ground, he had learned to say, "Do you want those piano keys shoved up your ass?" Half joke/half threat. He'd been a good wrestler, winning a state championship when he was seventeen. He accepted a full athletic scholarship at the University of Texas, but dislocated his shoulder his freshman year. Which, in retrospect, suited him just fine. At the age of nineteen, he was bored with wrestling. It had been a good thing to learn for a boy. It gave him confidence. He could learn some moves that could help him in a fight, learn not to panic when another man is trying to drive his head into the ground. And, if he was truly smart, learn how to avoid a fight, learn how to defuse situations before they became fights. Still, after high school, what was the point of wrestling? A lot of work and no glory. A handful of wrestlers in the nation might go to the Olympics. The rest would linger in obscurity, watching the girls walk off with the football and basketball players . . . watching in tights.

He moved from the piano into his den and returned to his senses.

He thought of Jamie Flatt. Interesting, attractive woman. Lovely body, a dancer's body. Like Rita Hayworth. He wondered if she knew who that was. Then he wondered what she'd look like dancing around a room like Rita Hayworth in *Gilda,* kicking up one of those long legs and bringing it down slowly. He thought about that for a while. Yeah . . . an interesting woman. He pressed the whiskey glass against his forehead.

She would come by in the morning and sign the affidavit and maybe help bring this awful mess to an end. He would give the affidavit to Martin and encourage him to release it to the newspapers. And the pressure to investigate Sam Clay would ratchet up a couple more notches.

But what about this Lieutenant Van?

Who was he? What role, if any, did he have in this?

Jamie said she had talked to him the night Carol was murdered. She said she had told him the chief was harassing her and could he please talk to him about it? The chief of police harasses a barmaid at a strip club . . . and the barmaid asks a patrol lieutenant to handle it. It didn't make any sense. Why would she do that? Was it because she didn't understand chain of command? Because she mistakenly believed a patrol lieutenant was on an equal management level with the chief? Was she ignorant or crazy?

No . . . she didn't seem to be either. She seemed to be pretty sharp actually. Perceptive and insightful. So if she wasn't stupid or crazy, was the patrol lieutenant indeed in such a position of power? Did he possess the ability to look the chief in the eye and say: you need to listen to what I'm saying.

Where would a patrol lieutenant get that sort of power?

How would he get it?

Jamie said the lieutenant lined up girls for the cops, including the chief.

Including the chief.

Chief Sam Clay bedding down with prostitutes? Kessler smiled at the thought. How could a public official do such a thing?

But social mores were a funny thing. Turn on a television and watch a typical contemporary sitcom. Jokes about oral sex and sodomy are common. Things are said that couldn't possibly be said as little as fifteen years ago. When he was a kid, "Three's Company" had been considered controversial even though none of the three characters ever seemed to get laid and the main guy only *pretended* to be gay. As the British comedians say, try telling that to the young people today, and they won't believe you. They won't. They can't because they're getting a steady media feeding of double entendres about masturbation and fellatio. It's not possible for them to understand that, at one time, you just couldn't say that on television. They've seen women on "The View" make jokes about 69 at ten o'clock in the morning.

Yet, Kessler thought, the 'fifties, 'sixties, and 'seventies were undoubtedly more licentious. Johnny Carson smoked and drank on his show while he joked about his ex-wives draining him. Angie Dickinson appeared naked in B movies. Politicians regularly slept with prostitutes and did not go to great lengths to conceal it either. And country club adultery was commonplace. But then the baby boomers took over all the institutions and made everything so damn puritanical.

1965: A police chief who spends a night at a brothel may joke about it the next day at the station.

2005: A police chief who does it might be in trouble.

Might be worried that people will find out that he "violated the public trust."

Might be blackmailed.

Things change and things stay the same, Kessler thought. Sex, blackmail. Power.

He had thought the chief had sent the renegade cop to kill him. But now he wasn't so sure. Maybe the lieutenant had had something to do with it. Or maybe the chief directed the lieutenant to send the patrol officer after him. If the chief were the one running the show, the City of Tulsa would be little better than a banana republic. A police state. That was an expression they tossed around a lot in law school classrooms and ACLU meetings. But the average person doesn't give much thought to it until he encounters government lawyers and prosecutors and cops willing to lie under oath. It's then that the conservative Republican becomes the civil rights liberal. It's then that the prospect of a bona-fide police state scares the hell out of him. Who will police the police? they say.

A fair question, but then their defenders come back and say, wait a minute. Get rid of these guys you call pigs, and who will serve and protect your ungrateful ass? How is a society going to function without its police? Care to live in some libertarian wonderland where everybody has to carry high-powered firearms and surround their homes with barbed wire fences? You want a society where ultimately the strong are given the freedom to oppress the weak?

Kessler remembered when, as a college student, he took a

trip to New York with a buddy and stayed out drinking till three in the morning. They had stumbled on to the subway, missed their stop, got off at 110th and Lenox, and walked straight up into Harlem. Terrifying, stupid mistake . . . two middle-class white boys wearing shorts and UT sweatshirts that might just as well have had bull's-eyes painted on them. But there were angels there to protect them. Three in fact, wearing blue uniforms with NYPD insignia—one white, two black. One of them spotted the two idiots, rolled his eyes, and pointed his finger to the stairwell they'd just exited, saying, "Go back down the stairs, get on the Nine, take it back to a Hundred and third." The cops followed them down to the subway and stayed with them until they boarded the next train. Angels from heaven.

These men who were trying to kill him, trying to frame him— what were they? Were they angels too? Were they the same men?

Tarra looked at the man in khaki pants, gray T-shirt, and light parka and thought, what a white boy. Though she herself was white. He was about the most unhip guy she'd ever seen. Like he'd looked up the casual section in a Brooks Brothers catalog and dressed accordingly.

"Your wife out of town?" she said.

Kessler hesitated nervously and said, "Does it show?"

"Yeah," she said, "it shows."

They were in a small room at the back of Cassy's. There was a small bed in the corner and not much else.

Tarra smiled at the man, thinking he was cute, in a clumsy sort of way. He reminded her of Inspector Clouseau, horny but gentle and awkward. She pulled her dress over her head and then shook her hair this way and that. It got him going, as she knew it would. She stood there in her red lace bra and panties.

She put her hands behind her head, hefting her breasts up.

"You like what you see?" she said.

Kessler could only say that he did.

She reached up behind to unhook her bra.

Kessler raised his hand to stop her. It wasn't easy.

"Hold it for a second, okay?"

Tarra thought, here we go. I've never done this before and do you mind if we talk first, I love my wife, but blah, blah, blah. And then she'd have to reply with something stupid like, it's okay, honey, there's nothing to it, and so forth. Not that she cared if he went through with it one way or the other; ride or no ride, he wasn't getting his 200 bucks back. But it was easier when they didn't try to back out. Get him through it, and he'll enjoy himself then feel bad and return in about ten days, telling his wife he'll be working late.

But the guy said, "I'm sorry. Van told me I shouldn't be nervous."

Tarra said, "Why should you be nervous?"

"Well, the law . . ."

"Honey, ain't no laws being broken here. You wearing a wire or something?" She was smiling when she said it.

"No," Kessler said, thinking if he wasn't careful she'd find out he was being truthful, and soon. "Do you know Van?"

"You ask too many questions," she said. She took off her top and walked to him, put her arms around him and kissed on the neck. Holding herself close now. "Oh," she said, "nothing wrong with you, junior."

Kessler lightly pushed her back. "Easy," he said.

"Come on," she said. "What are you, a minister or something? You don't look like a minister." Then whispered something in his ear that would have made Larry Flynt blush.

And Kessler thought, oh man . . . what am I doing here? . . . The lieutenant. That's right. Lieutenant Van. He was supposed to be finding out what his connections were to this place . . . this prostitution ring . . . but it didn't seem to be working and he was in real danger of giving new meaning to the expression *pump for information.*

"Oh, that sounds . . . interesting," he said. "But I think I've changed my mind."

"Come on," she said.

". . . No."

"Come on," she whispered.

"No."

She stepped back from him, cold suddenly. "Well, don't ask for your money back, 'cause you ain't gonna get it."

Kessler said, "I'm not asking."

"Then what's the problem?" she said. "You're not a fag obviously."

Kessler thought, what was the problem? Well, it was illegal. But apart from that, it didn't take a genius to see that this sort of thing could be habit-forming. He could lie down and get what he paid for. But if he did, he'd probably come back and if she wasn't here, he'd likely ask what else they had on tap. There was a little Charlie Sheen in the best of men, and he knew it.

"Adios," he said. And walked out.

He got out of the door in time and walked down the long, dank corridor, thinking: well, that was useless. Then came out into the main showroom and walked to the bar. The whole place was bathed in a cold, dark red. Air conditioning blasting, though it was probably in the sixties outside. Poor girls on the stage must be freezing their heinies off.

The bartender asked him what he wanted and he asked for a Bushmills on ice.

"We don't have that," the bartender said.

"Give me a Jack Daniel's on ice then," Kessler said.

A couple of minutes later the bartender returned with a beer mug filled to the top with ice and whiskey. Kessler paid the man, regarded the mug with curiosity and shook his head. Not the most sophisticated topless bar he'd ever been in. But it was a whorehouse too. Should that make a difference? Was there such a thing as a sophisticated brothel? They seemed to have such things in European films. Hollywood, on the other hand, loved to make movies about the golden-hearted whore. But the prostitutes he'd seen didn't look anything like Julia Roberts or Jamie Lee Curtis. Some of the ones you saw on Eleventh Street looked more like Tony Curtis.

Tarra had been attractive in a cheap sort of way. Nice figure, to be sure. But with a strung-out, tired expression on her face. She couldn't have been more than twenty-two.

"How's your drink, partner?"

Kessler looked up to see a man with a thin mustache.

"It's fine," Kessler said. If you drink like Babe Ruth. But then thought, why dink with the guy? He seemed harmless enough. A thin, Southern-looking guy with his thin mustache, wearing clothes that looked like they had just been pressed. Probably the manager or the owner.

"Monty," the bartender called out. "You got a phone call."

"Who is it?"

The bartender said, "Van."

The man the bartender called Monty said, "Excuse me," and left Kessler alone.

Kessler watched him as he picked up the phone. He couldn't hear what the man was saying on the phone, so he slid off his stool and walked closer to him. He kept his back to the bar and his eyes on the stage where the girls danced.

Monty said, "Now? . . . I don't know . . . I understand that . . . I understand that . . . all right, all right . . . I'll be there in about fifteen. . . . Yeah . . . See you then."

There was some movement behind him and soon Kessler heard Monty tell the bartender, "I've got to run an errand. I should be back in an hour."

★ ★ ★ ★ ★

Kessler followed Monty, tailing the guy's Lincoln Continental in the Buick LeSabre. To the Broken Arrow Expressway and then north on Peoria Avenue through the upper part of the city until the city drifted away behind them and the street became Highway 11. They passed dirty fields and junkyards and then they were in a small town called Turley.

Monty pulled the Lincoln Continental into the parking lot of a convenience store that was closed.

Kessler pulled into the far south side of the lot, behind a row of parked cars.

He waited and watched as Monty got out and walked to the front of the convenience store. A bearded guy came out from the shadows. The bearded man wore jeans and cowboy boots. A handsome guy, with a lean, tough look. A little bit like Hank . . . more expensive clothes though and concerned with his looks in a way Hank wouldn't be. The man was not wearing a uniform, but Kessler figured it was Lieutenant Van.

The two men spoke for a couple of minutes and then Monty walked over to a pay phone to make a call. He was on the phone for maybe half a minute, then he hung up and both men got into the Lincoln. The car started and backed out of its space.

Kessler thought, follow them or don't follow them? Follow them where? To their secret hideout? Another waste of time, trying to play detective. He started the Buick, thinking he had to go back to town anyway . . . just as well drive behind them. He drove the Buick forward, past the row of cars and then behind the convenience store, rolled in the dark backlot past empty milk crates and trash Dumpsters, then swung left to come out on the northern end of the store.

Then stomped on the brakes.

To his left, parked next to the convenience store, was Carol's Volvo station wagon.

Twenty-Six

When he had last seen the car, it had been backing out of his driveway. Quickly. Though not quickly enough for him at the time. He had stood on his porch watching it leave, wishing he'd never met her, hoping he'd never see her again. Thinking, *go and don't come back.* Thinking, *get your fucking car out of my driveway.*

The woman was dead now, he thought. Satisfied?

And here was her car.

Probably dropped off by Lieutenant Van.

Why?

Last Wednesday, someone had killed her and put her body in the trunk of his car. Probably while he was asleep in his own house. Maybe if he'd had a dog, it would have heard men stealing around his driveway and barked up a storm and fouled up their plans. But he didn't have a dog and they had placed a corpse in his car as easily as throwing an egg on it.

But they hadn't left *her* car there. They hadn't left her car at his house.

Why not?

If they had done that, then what?

If they had left her car at his house, he would have seen it first thing Thursday morning and thought, hello? What is Carol's car doing here? And he might've reported it. Might've reported her missing to the police. And if he had done that, the police would have probably found Carol in his car.

But if that had happened Thursday morning, he wouldn't have been shot at Thursday night. If her car was discovered too early, they wouldn't have the opportunity to kill him.

Ergo, the men who put the body in his car did not want him discovered that morning. Which meant that the men who sent the patrol officer to kill him were the same men who moved this car.

And here it was. Not fifteen feet from him.

Sitting in the Buick, Kessler thought, leave it. Leave it and get out of here.

It could well have been that Monty had just used that pay phone to call the police and report an abandoned Volvo wagon, license plate KAY-441. Which would eventually bring detectives and OSBI investigators roaring up to this lot. They showed up and saw him here, he'd have some 'splaining to do. And as usual the truth wouldn't cut it. He'd tell them he followed a pimp here and saw him meet an off-duty cop who was trying to frame him, and they'd nod sympathetically as they clapped the cuffs on him.

Leave it and go.

Kessler said, "Shit." He stuck the column shift into park, got out, and walked over to the Volvo.

It was locked of course.

He peered through the windows, wondering if he'd see another dead body. Maybe Sam Clay's for some reason. But there was nobody inside. It was empty and clean. Nothing of any interest.

And then he saw it.

A silver glint on the floor in front of the passenger seat.

A gun.

No. Not a gun. More like a piece of pipe or a crowbar . . .

His heart jumped in horror. And he half walked, half ran back to the Buick. He got a flashlight out of the glove compartment and came back to the Volvo and shined the light into the car.

And then he knew.

The thing on the floor was a tire iron. A tool used to twist the lug nuts off a wheel. It had a red stain on one end of it. And the distinct BMW trademark on the other. He'd only had a flat tire once, had only used the tool once, but he knew it when he saw it. He knew it belonged to him.

He said, "You mother—"

Then he heard the sirens in the distance.

Distant, but audible. Maybe going to the site of a car wreck or a house fire. Or maybe responding to an anonymous tip placed from the pay phone a few feet away.

Do something, Kessler thought. Move. And he stopped thinking and moved . . . to the side of the convenience store where there was a metal trash can. He picked it up and began moving toward the Volvo, but knew as soon as he hefted it, it wouldn't have the sufficient mass to do the job and like that threw it on the ground . . . and hurried over to a place where five or six gray cinderblocks were stacked against the wall. Using both hands, he picked one up and heaved it through the passenger-side window.

Before doing that, he wasn't sure if he heard the police sirens drawing nearer. But after smashing the window, those sounds were instantly overcome by the sound of the car's burglar alarm. It was European-made and it made a noise that went, "*THWEEP!*, *THWEEP!*, *THWEEP!*, *THWEEP!*," piercing the night.

Kessler reached in and unlocked the door. He opened it up and grabbed the tire iron. Then walked quickly to the Buick and drove off the convenience store lot. A few yards down, he made a left turn on to the main road and soon passed a caravan of police cars—three of them—going in the opposite direction.

He kept driving south on Highway 11, keeping the Buick under the speed limit.

A few minutes later, he felt better.

He drove to Lake Skiatook and got rid of the tire iron. Another lake, he thought. He was going to run out of lakes.

TWENTY-SEVEN

They talked about Carol's disappearance again on the ten o'clock news. There was nothing to add to the story, but they brought it up anyway. *Still Missing,* the banner read, under a picture of her that was about five years old. A few days now and the media was becoming more and more convinced she had been murdered. So was the OSBI.

Sam Clay turned off the television and thought about it. He was alone in his house, no place to go. Nobody to see, nobody who wanted to see him. He didn't know if he'd ever felt so alone. There had always been someone there to stand by him. Not out of love or affection, but usually out of ambition or fear. An assistant, a captain who wanted to be the next assistant chief, a lackey who hoped to be his full-time driver. People to remind him who he was and what position he held.

He could have used someone like that today. When an OSBI investigator named Claude Lovett had called him.

The investigator had been no one special, just a mid-level agent. The OSBI didn't even have the decency to have its director call him first, if only just to warn him. Hadn't he deserved that? Granted, the OSBI had a job to do. But couldn't they have had the director call him and tell him the investigator's request for a statement was only a formality? Didn't he deserve at least that much respect? Claude Lovett . . . who the hell was he? Sounded like a west Okie farmer.

Lovett had said, "Chief, I understand you're a busy man. But

I was hoping we could arrange a time for me to ask you just a few questions."

And Sam had said, using the voice of authority, "About what?"

"About your wife, sir," the investigator had said, not backing down a bit. The insolent son of a bitch.

"My wife is my concern."

"Yes, sir. We all want to do everything we can." Then, "Can we meet tomorrow?"

"Who are you?"

"As I said before, sir. Agent Claude Lovett of the OSBI. I've been assigned to do the preliminary investigation."

"Well, Agent Lovett, you don't just call me at my office in the middle of the afternoon and tell me I need to give you a statement. It doesn't work that way."

"You hired a lawyer?"

"What?"

"Have you hired a lawyer?"

"No. Why should I?"

"Then how should it work?"

"You . . . you go through chain of command. You go through the proper channels, officer."

"Yes, sir. But this is not an administrative investigation. This is a criminal investigation."

Sam was furious. No cop had spoken to him like that in twenty years. He had said, "You don't have the right to talk to me like that. It's unprofessional. I know your boss Frank Rundgren and I know he won't be pleased to hear that you've talked to me this way."

"Sir, I'm acting on Mr. Rundgren's orders. If you want to call him, you're welcome to do so."

"I will," Sam had said and slammed down the phone.

Then thought, what the hell is going on? He knew Frank

Rundgren. Frank was a nice guy. Why would he allow this farmer to speak to him like he was a street pimp? Why was he letting this happen? Did Frank think he was guilty? That he'd killed his wife? He couldn't possibly believe that. Could he? Frank was a cop too, and now he was abandoning him. It was cowardly and unprofessional. It was a gutless betrayal.

It was the lawyer's fault. That damn lawyer leaking his interview to the press and telling the world that Carol had been afraid of him. Insinuating that he'd threatened to kill her. It was a filthy goddamned lie. It was slander. He'd never threatened her. Certainly, he'd never threatened to kill her. And she'd never really been afraid of him. Maybe if she had, this whole thing would not have happened. If she feared him, she wouldn't have messed around on him and started it all.

It was an *accident,* goddammit. It was an accident. He was no murderer. And now this lawyer, this lawyer who fucked his wife, was telling everyone that he was a wife beater and saying send the murderer to jail. The guy had no shame. He was nothing but a goddamn liar. Like all lawyers. Open their mouths and the lies just come tumbling out. They lied and lied and they felt no compunction about doing it. No one called lawyers pigs. Yet they lie and twist things and the people buy it. People believed that he killed Carol. People like the mayor. People like Frank Rundgren. Or, if they didn't believe he did, they weren't going to come near him until he was cleared. It wasn't right. It just wasn't right.

And now, on top of everything, the city attorney had told him he needed to think about getting his own attorney. In other words, the city would not be furnishing him with one. In his capacity of chief, he had been sued a number of times. Usually they were civil rights cases. When these suits were filed, the city always paid for his lawyer. Now he'd been told he'd have to pay for his own. Was that fair? A lawyer leaks some lies to the press and now he has to pay for his own attorney?

He'd never had to pay for his own attorney before. Even when he divorced his first wife, they had done it all by agreement. No attorney, no attorney fees. He wondered now if he should have stayed with Shirley. She was a stupid, fat woman . . . uneducated, unsophisticated, talked loudly to waiters if her food was cold. His high school girl that he'd married before he even finished college. Why? . . . After college, he'd joined the Houston Police Department and eventually rose to the position of deputy chief. He left there to take the chief's position in Tulsa. Lived his entire life in two cities. But when he left the first town, he decided he would leave the life that went with it. He didn't love Shirley and he doubted she loved him. And he saw no reason to make her the wife of a police chief. She was hurt by his decision to divorce her, but partly relieved by it.

In Tulsa, he met Carol Macy at a political fund-raiser. She was also recently divorced. They began dating and married seven months later. Carol was everything he thought he wanted. She was intelligent, educated, ambitious, and good-looking. She was what a man like him deserved. But after a couple of years, he realized there had been a trade-off. His first wife was none of the things Carol was; in fact, she probably hadn't even liked him very much. But she never crossed him. She never undermined him. She never acted as if she were smarter than him. Carol did. Indirectly, perhaps. But she did all those shitty things all the same. A look, a glance, a sardonic way of saying "really?"—all ways of telling him she thought he was a fool. Always belittling him.

He did not believe that he'd meant to kill Carol. It had been an accident, he told himself. But part of him was glad she was dead.

He wished Paul Kessler was dead too.

The telephone rang.

Sam picked it up. "Hello."

"Sam."

It was Van.

The chief said, "What is it?"

"I think we're okay now. They're going to find Carol's car." Van said, "Listen for it on your scanner."

"Tonight?"

"Yeah. Tonight."

The chief said, "You better hope so."

There was a silence on the other end of the line and for a moment, the chief thought Van had hung up. But then heard him say, "Sam, you don't want to threaten me."

Twenty-Eight

Van hung up the phone and handed it to a waitress to put it back behind the bar. He took a few seconds to cool off.

Buddy Matlock was sitting at the table with him. Unlike Van, he was in uniform. He said, "Everything okay?"

Van said, "He's nervous."

Buddy said, "You blame him?"

"I worry about him," Van said. "He's forgetting who his friends are."

They were at Cassy's. Last call, Monday night. The girls had left the stage. They had turned off the music and there was a baseball game on television.

Buddy said, "He's too used to being in charge."

"We are talking about the chief here, aren't we?"

Buddy and Van turned to see Kessler standing next to their table. Like he had just walked up. Van recognized him right away, but didn't show it, keeping his expression calm. He glanced at Buddy and Buddy looked like he was ready to skin his leather right then and there, and Van thought, Jesus, man, not here. Not now. And he reached out and lightly touched Buddy on the arm. Steady.

Van said, "Excuse me?"

Kessler said, "You were talking about Sam, weren't you?"

"Sam . . . Sam who?" Van said.

"Sam Clay," Kessler said. "That's Chief Sam Clay to you." And then . . . sat down . . . ? . . . and said, "Or is it? Maybe it's just plain Sam." Looking right at Van now.

Van almost smiled. The guy had balls, trying to psyche him. Sitting at their table uninvited. Van said, "Do I know you, friend?"

"Yeah. I think you do."

Van made a curious expression and leaned forward to study him. He frowned and said, "No, I don't think so. Any reason I should recognize you?"

Kessler shrugged. "My picture's been in the paper."

"Still not registering," Van said. "One thing I do know: you're not a cop."

Buddy said, "And this is a cop's place."

"Yeah," Kessler said, "that's what I hear. Everybody comes to Van's."

Van said, "Now who would go and tell you something like that?"

Kessler said, "Carol Macy."

"Is that right?" Van said. Then mock surprise. "Hey, you *have* been in the papers. You're the guy that she was sleeping with."

"I thought it might come to you."

Van said, "Buddy, this is the fellah that says the police are conspiring to frame him for murder. Recognize him now?"

Buddy didn't say anything.

"Mr. Conspiracy," Van said, "You know anything about psychology?"

"A little," Kessler said.

"Then you should know what all conspiracy nuts have in common," Van said. "Paranoia. We know a lot about that in our business. See, the problem with the paranoid is his ego. He thinks he's really important. He believes that everybody knows who he is and nobody has anything better to do than spend their time trying to ruin his life. They see themselves at the center of the universe. But the truth is, nobody cares about the paranoid's life as much as the paranoid. It's a delusion. A belief that people like me give a flying fuck about people like you, one way or the other. The problem is, friend, we don't. We don't even know you."

Kessler said, "You know, I'm inclined to agree. The paranoid basically being self-absorbed. You're right about that. A man can get so caught up in the events of his life, he starts to think that those events are the only thing that matter. To anyone. So what does Sam Clay have on you?"

"Pardon?"

"What is it that Sam Clay has on you that he could get you involved in this?"

Van had been caught off guard. The man had talked philosophical shit and almost got him to let down his defenses. He gathered himself and said, "Are you high?"

Kessler went on as if he hadn't heard him. "I've thought about it the last few days, this problem. You might even say it's been kinda gnawing at me. I thought, why would regular patrol cops go out of their way to fuck over some guy who'd bedded down with the chief's wife? What would they gain? Why would they do that? I suppose it could be because Sam Clay's a fellow cop. But that doesn't really make sense. Because Sam's not really a cop after all. He's a politician. He's brass. He's not one of you. And if things were the other way around, say if it were Officer Matlock here that had killed his wife, the chief wouldn't lift a finger to help him. He'd sell the street cop out in a heartbeat. I don't know a whole lot about cop culture, but I know that much. So I wondered: why would you do for him what he wouldn't do for you? And then I thought: of course, Sam Clay knows something about these fellows. And they know he knows. They know if he's busted, they'll be at risk too." Kessler said, "So you're right. It really isn't about me, is it? It's about you."

Van said, "Man, that's quite a theory. You think it's going to keep you out of jail?"

"That's to find out."

"Yeah, well," Van said, "you'll need some proof to support that theory. And I got a feeling you don't have any."

"We do what we can," Kessler said. "Sometimes that means testifying to the things dead people have told us. People like Carol. And Officer Miller."

Kessler thought he saw Matlock flinch and he tensed himself in case the cop pulled his nightstick.

Van lowered his voice and leaned closer to Kessler. "Friend," he said, "it's not smart to slander an officer killed in the line of duty. Not here."

Kessler said, "He was loyal to you, I suppose. But he was a bit of a fuck-up, wasn't he?"

Buddy rushed him, but Kessler was ready, stepping out of his chair before the cop could get on him. They faced off, Kessler keeping his eyes on the man's nightstick. Maybe he would be able to deflect the strike if it came, maybe he wouldn't. But it didn't come because the lieutenant was ordering Buddy to chill and stand down. The three men remained on their feet for a few tense moments, and then Buddy put his nightstick back in his belt and walked to the bar.

Kessler felt no gratitude toward the lieutenant because he knew he had not restrained Matlock to protect him. He'd only done it to protect himself. Vannerson had planted the tire iron and he expected a warrant to be issued for Kessler's arrest by morning. He didn't want a brawl to get in the way of that.

"You've got a big mouth," Van said.

"And you're a fucking idiot," Kessler said. "Not a good thing for a cop to be when he's dirty. You probably could've gotten away with your nickel-and-dime pimp bullshit until you retired. But you weren't satisfied with that. You had to form an alliance with Sam Clay and prove to him that you were a player. Well, I know all about him, lieutenant. He's not the most stable guy on the block. He's gonna get popped, and when he does, he's gonna take you down with him."

It took Van a moment to process it. He wanted to respond, but the man had turned his back and walked. Van reached down and rested his hand on his service weapon as his eyes picked out a spot on Kessler's back. Skin it, he thought. Pull it out and put three shots in the man's back. Think up an excuse later, but put him down . . . Now . . . *now* . . .

But there were too many witnesses . . . Other people in the bar, bartenders and waitresses, there was no time to think it out . . . and then the man was at the door . . . and out. Gone.

Van took his hand off his Glock.

Van decided he needed a drink, so he went to the bar and got a bottle of Budweiser. Popped the top and sucked about a third of it down. Then stopped and thought, shit, drinking on duty. Christ, the lawyer was getting to him now. If he wasn't careful, Buddy would see it and start to think he was losing his nerve. He poured the remainder of the beer down the sink and threw the empty bottle in the trash.

Buddy came up and stood on the other side of the bar. "Why did you let him go, Van?"

"Where's he gonna go?" Van said. He could not let Buddy think he'd even thought about shooting Kessler just now, couldn't have him think he was indecisive or desperate. Van said, "Tomorrow afternoon he'll be arrested."

"But the things he said," Buddy said. "How could he know?"

"He's bluffing."

"I don't know, Van," Buddy said. "He seemed to know a lot. Maybe Clay's wife . . . what do you think?"

"How the hell should I know what she told him?" Van said. "Didn't I just tell you he's going to be arrested."

"Yeah, but is that going to be enough?"

"It'll be enough," Van said. Though he wasn't sure himself anymore. So he began to talk it out, as though to convince himself. "A man gets arrested," Van said, "and people will presume he's guilty. That's the way it really works. Guilt is presumed until you're proven innocent. And how's he gonna prove he's innocent? By arguing he was framed by cops? Who will believe him?"

"I suppose you're right," Buddy said.

And then Van thought, hey, maybe he was right. And he felt better. So he asked Buddy to have a beer with him. And then another. And pretty soon, he wondered what he'd been so damn rattled about. The guy was just a punk and a bigmouth. A smooth talker, sure, but no different than any other turd they'd dealt with.

His good mood held until Monty told him there was a call for him.

Van said into the phone, "Yeah."

"It seems you fucked up again."

It was Sam.

Twenty-Nine

When Claude Lovett was a young beat cop for the Oklahoma City Police Department, he'd earned the nickname "Roger." As in Roger Staubach, quarterback of the then Dallas Cowboys.

It happened this way:

Out on patrol, he pulled over a carload of gangbangers riding in a Chevy Caprice with a busted taillight. Four of them got out and stood in a line like so many Rockettes. Claude was riding alone that night. He took their driver's licenses and phoned them in on his handheld police radio. Dispatch radioed him back to tell him that one of the young fellows was wanted for questioning in a murder investigation. The young man in question heard the dispatcher's squawk too and took off running. Quickly, Claude threw his handheld at the fleeing suspect. The handheld radios at that time were heavy, clunky Motorolas that weighed about the same as a large can of Maxwell House coffee. The radio caught the suspect square in the back of the head and sent him sprawling to the ground. Even the suspect's friends were impressed by Claude's precision, and did not hesitate to obey when Claude pulled his other service weapon and ordered them to put their hands on the patrol car.

He eventually transferred to the detective division and became a lieutenant. At the age of fifty-two, having completed his twenty years, he drew his state pension and retired from the OCPD. Within a year, fearing he would die of boredom, he signed up with the Oklahoma State Bureau of Investigation and became a special agent, investigating insurance fraud, mostly, and other mundane things. He liked the OSBI, liked its pace and workload. Though he promised his wife he'd only stay there five years. One year left now. After that, he'd begin serving his sentence of roaming about the country in a thirty-foot recreational vehicle, visiting grandchildren. Lord.

He was not a slick-looking man. He was short and stocky, with a stomach hanging over his belt. He had thick gray hair and a mustache, and his clothes were unfashionable. In short, he looked like a cop. People saw the cheap golf shirts and the baggy pants and the white socks and thought, looky here, it's Country Willie. And when they so underestimated him, he was halfway home. He was a wily detective and a shrewd investigator, and he didn't miss much.

Now he stood by the Volvo station wagon with the smashed window, wondering why it had taken this long for them to find Judge Macy's car. Here and there, his face was illuminated by the flash of a camera, police photographer at work.

Nearby stood one of his assistants, OSBI Agent Coy Russell, chewing gum.

Behind him was Captain Devereaux of the Tulsa police.

Devereaux had been a little cool to Claude when they first met, but had warmed a little since. Claude Lovett couldn't yet tell where Devereaux's sympathies were, whether they were with the chief or the integrity of the investigation. But Devereaux was the Tulsa PD liaison and they would need his cooperation for the time being.

Captain Devereaux said, "I don't know. Maybe nobody noticed it until tonight."

Agent Russell said, "That make sense?"

"No," Devereaux said, "it doesn't make *sense*. But it's an explanation." Coy Russell was just shy of thirty, and Devereaux gave Lovett a look that said, I know I'm in a subordinate role here, but do I really have to take smack from this punk?

Claude saw the point and said, "Yes, it's an explanation. Mal, you think someone may have moved the car here tonight?" Being diplomatic.

"It's possible," Devereaux said. "It may even be likely."

"Maybe the same guy brought the car here that made the call," Claude said. "Maybe. But that wouldn't explain this smashed window."

Coy Russell said, "Smash and grab?"

"Grabbed what?" Claude said.

Devereaux shook his head. "There's nothing missing."

Coy Russell shrugged. "The car alarm scared the guy off."

"The alarm was still going when the first patrol cars arrived here," Claude said. "Which means . . . what? It was set off after the phone call was placed." He gestured toward the pay phone. "From there. Where was Clay tonight?" He looked at Devereaux as he said it.

Devereaux said, "I don't know. It could have been him that moved the car here. We can check. Has he agreed to be interviewed by you?"

Claude shook his head. "I doubt he will. He'll probably hire an attorney by tomorrow. And a good one'll advise him to invoke the Fifth." Claude said, "What do you think?"

Devereaux said, "I think you're right."

"What about the boyfriend?" Claude said.

"The lawyer?"

"Yeah."

"He might have brought it here," Devereaux said. "We can check him out. It's up to you."

Yes, it is, Claude thought. He'd have Coy investigate the lawyer's whereabouts tomorrow. Maybe the lawyer's lawyer would answer, maybe he wouldn't.

Devereaux said it then, point blank, "Which do you suspect?

The boyfriend or the husband?"

Claude said, "Everyone and no one." Let him chew on that for a while.

THIRTY

Van paid his seven bucks, picked up his ticket and walked into the theater.

It was one of those cineplexes on the south side that had twenty screens inside, three of them showing the new Ben Affleck action film, *Dead in the Water*. The billboards showed that Ben was playing a cop, for the first time apparently, wearing a three-day beard and untucked shirt and carrying a Sig Sauer automatic, holding it with both hands toward the ground like he was hunting mice or something . . . doing their best to market the guy as the next Bruce Willis. Van sighed. Ben Affleck shooting a bunch of Norwegian supercriminals. It was inevitable, he supposed. Most of the regular action heroes—Eastwood, Stallone, Willis—they were too old to play the Cop-on-the-Edge roles anymore and Mel Gibson had gotten all holy. The next generation had to take over at some point.

Like most cops, Van was aware of how unrealistic cop action movies were. And like most cops, Van loved these movies all the same. In a typical twenty-year career, maybe one policeman in a hundred would shoot and kill someone on duty. The odds of shooting ten to twelve perps in a three-day period was infinitesimal. They just didn't give you that kind of opportunity. The real life had some excitement, some physical risk. But not much. There was danger all right, but not the kind that comes from fighting with some guy on top of a moving train. That kind would be easier to deal with than the reality. It was the steady, everyday dangers that would do you in. The daily experience of witnessing human nature's abundant, unceasing cruelty that will weaken the strongest man. Combine that with the boredom and the paranoia and you've got a real psychological hazard. They needed the movies, needed the escape. At times, more so than the civilians.

Yeah, it was a stressful life. Even more so when you added the prospect of going to jail.

He found the men's room and went in. He walked to the urinal and relieved himself. Then walked to the sink to wash his hands. He studied himself in the mirror.

He didn't look stressed. That was good. He was holding together rather well, considering. He wasn't going down. Not for this. He would be fine.

He said to the mirror, "How long you been here?"

Dave Mayfield said, "Twenty minutes, give or take. I decided to come early this time."

Van turned around to face the man. "All this distrustfulness," Van said.

Mayfield said, "What did you want to see me about?"

Van said, "We've got a problem."

"We do?"

"Yeah," Van said. "Have you heard about Chief Clay?"

"I read a little bit about it," Mayfield said. "His wife disappeared?"

"Yeah, a few days ago." Van said, "She had something going with this lawyer friend of hers, and they're looking into him. But I think they're going to be checking on the chief too."

Mayfield said, "You think he killed her?"

"Who?"

"The chief," Mayfield said. "You think he killed her?"

Van said, "I don't know. He might have."

Mayfield smiled and said, "You know, you said 'we' earlier."

"So?"

"So, when a black man hears 'we,' he gets suspicious." Mayfield said, "Like, 'we've got to get this yard cleaned up' means, nigger, get this yard cleaned up."

Van said, "What's your point?"

"My point is, lieutenant, why are you saying 'we' when it's your problem?"

Hell, Van thought, laying the black guy shit on him again. But he had been ready for this. Of course, he couldn't tell Mayfield everything. But he needed to tell him some things. It would need to be a careful mixture of truth and deceit. Van said, "Well, I have reason to believe the chief may want to cut a deal. He may want to help bring down some cops he thinks are dirty. And in exchange, they'll go easy on him."

Mayfield said, "You have 'reason to believe,' huh?"

Van said, "Yes."

"Van, I'm not entirely sure you're being straight with me."

"Why's that?"

"Well," Mayfield said, "you say you think the chief *might* have killed his wife. But then you talk about him cutting deals with the district attorney. Now, why would he do that if he didn't kill her?"

Van said, "I don't know."

"Come on, Van. Don't tell me you don't know," Mayfield said. "We're supposed to be friends. Don't talk to me like a lawyer. Tell me what you really think."

"Okay," Van said. "I think the chief killed her."

"Now that's better," Mayfield said. "Now, these dirty cops you talk about, that wouldn't include a Lieutenant Greg Vannerson, would it?"

"What the fuck's that supposed to mean?"

"Hey, Greg," Mayfield said, "it's just me. That expression—'dirty'—that's from your world, man, not mine. I don't think of

207

you that way. I think of you as a man. That's all. But let's talk about what we're talking about. Okay?"

Van let himself cool down. Then he said, "The chief knows things about me . . . he knows about me having parties for other cops. At Cassy's. You know it?"

"I know it," Mayfield said.

"Well, there are girls at these parties. Call girls. The chief's taken a piece himself a couple of times. He might give that up if they come after him."

Mayfield said, "You set up these parties?"

"Yes."

Mayfield smiled. "Van," he said, "you in the girl business?"

"No," Van said. "It's for the men. I'm not a pimp."

Mayfield ignored the evasion. He said, "Van, the ladies' Man. What you gonna do next, cut a rap CD?"

"That's very funny."

"But, Van," Mayfield said, "the chief doesn't know about our business, does he?"

"No," Van said. "But the point is, if they investigate me for Cassy's, they're liable to investigate me for the I-44 rest stop. They're going to start asking about Marcus Wells."

Mayfield stared at Van for several moments. It made Van uncomfortable, but he tried not to read too much into it.

"Van," Mayfield said, "this sounds like your problem. You want to make it our problem?"

"Dave," Van said, using the man's first name for the first time, "let me be real clear about something: I am not threatening you. I wouldn't even think of doing something like that. I'm just telling you how it is."

"Huh," Mayfield said. "You mean you're worried about the chief for both our sakes. That it?"

"Yeah."

"Well," Mayfield said, "if you're that worried, why don't you just take care of it yourself?"

Van saw his meaning, but pretended he didn't.

"I don't follow you," he said.

"Yeah, you do."

"What do you mean?"

"Van, stop it," Mayfield said. "You want this man dead, don't you?"

Van realized then that to keep up the charade would be to insult the man. And if he did that, he'd lose him for sure. So he dropped it.

"Yeah," Van, "the chief needs to die."

Mayfield said, "Then kill him."

"I can't," Van said.

"Why not?" Mayfield said. "You've done it before."

"What are you talking about?"

"I'm talking about Marcus, Van. You're not going to tell me that wasn't a killing, are you? I shot him, but you left him there for me to shoot. What's the difference?"

"The difference is . . ." Van said. But he couldn't finish it.

"The difference in your mind is, Marcus was a nigger drug dealer," Mayfield said. "That's the difference."

"Hey, come on," Van said. "You don't know me. Why're you accusing me of thinking that?"

"Okay, you're not a racist," Mayfield said. "But do you see now what I was talking about earlier? Marcus didn't deserve it because of what he was or who he was. He was just unlucky, see? A fucked-up man in the wrong place at the wrong time. Isn't this chief of yours the same way?"

Van didn't see it that way at all. But he could see that he was going to have to concede the point. Otherwise, he'd receive no help at all.

"I suppose."

"Ain't no supposing about it," Mayfield said. "But I digress.

Are you saying you can't kill a man face to face?" Prodding him now.

"I can do it, same as you."

"Then do it," Mayfield said.

And like that, he was walking toward the door.

Van said, "Hey . . . wait."

Mayfield turned.

Van said, "Okay, I'll pay you for it."

"You'll pay me?" Mayfield said. "What have you got to pay me?"

"Sixty thousand," Van said. "The money I got from you."

"I gave you a hundred thousand."

"I split it with my men," Van said.

"You gave them twenty apiece?"

"They earned it."

"Well, that's admirable, Van," Mayfield said. "But sixty thousand's lunch money to me. And even if I needed it, think of the risk. One thing to kill a drug trafficker. It's another to kill a public official, especially one in law enforcement. Kill Marcus Wells and, within a week, he's forgotten. Kill the chief of police of a major metropolitan city, man, that sort of thing causes a panic. Citizens drive with their headlights on and look for someone to hang. You of all people know that. They'll call in everyone to investigate. Feds, state, and city. Everyone. And that sort of headache just ain't worth sixty thousand to me."

Van said, "Didn't you say killing the chief was no different than killing Marcus?"

"It isn't," Mayfield said. "But the risks are . . . Listen, Van, I'd like to help you. I really would. But you're going to have to handle this thing yourself."

He left and Van thought, lazy prick. He waited for fifteen minutes and then left the theater. Outside, a car pulled up and he got in.

Buddy said, "Well?"

"He won't do it," Van said.

"He won't do it?" Buddy said. "With all the shit we got on him? Man, we *make* him do it."

"We can make him do it, sure," Van said. "But he's so nervous he'll fuck it up. It's not that he won't do it. He can't."

Buddy seemed uncertain. He said, "The way he carries on?"

"That's an act," Van said. "Behind all that smooth jig bullshit, he's a coward. I'm telling you, we can't rely on him."

Buddy still seemed unsure, thinking back to the way Mayfield had so coolly iced one of his own men. He said, "What are we going to do then?"

Whatever they did, Van thought, they'd probably need to do it tonight. The chief had told him that they hadn't found the tire iron at the scene. Between all the yelling, that's what the chief had told him. Yelling, sure, but jumpy as hell. The chief was panicking, falling apart. Jesus, the lawyer had been right. The fucking lawyer. Playing me now, Van thought. Telling me that Sam would crack and then Sam calls, cracking. Sam was trying to sound tough, but he'd hire a lawyer by lunchtime tomorrow. And then he'd be gone, out of reach.

Lawyers. Paul Kessler, attorney-at-law and amateur mindfucker. Trying to psyche Van into going after Sam. Maybe even into killing Sam. That's probably what Kessler wanted, the fucking savage. Okay, slick, Van thought. You want me to kill Sam, maybe I will. Maybe I will and solve my problems. But don't think you're going to be left out of this. It ain't going to work that way.

"Van?"

"What?"

"What are we going to do?"

"Buddy," Van said, "I think all the parties involved in this thing need to get together. Sit down and discuss it. Have a little mediation."

"You mean bring Kessler and the chief together?"

"Yeah."

"Are you serious?" Buddy said. "Man, they're liable to kill each other."

Van said, "I think we can count on it."

Dave turned around to make sure Van wasn't following him, then slipped into a theater. He took a seat near the back and kept his eyes on the entrances for fifteen minutes. The time passed and then he decided he could relax and watch the movie.

It turned out to be something with Kevin Costner playing a college professor who was in danger of losing tenure because he was defending the university's blue-collar workers' right to form a union. Dave liked movies, and the plot of this one seemed to have some promise, but Costner didn't seem comfortable playing the part. Like he was yearning to return to some suck-ass apocalypse film so he could try to be Steve McQueen. The movie might have worked if they'd gotten Jimmy Woods to play the role, or maybe even Michael Douglas. Dave thought Costner was all right, basically, and didn't deserve all the ragging he got. But his stuff only seemed to work when he played losers. He should give up the McQueen thing. As far as Dave was concerned, McQueen was just about the coolest white man who ever lived and to try to be him was to set yourself up to look like a fool. A man should accept who he is.

He gave up when Costner got naked and climbed in the shower with one of his idealistic coeds, muttered, "That's all I can take," walked out to the lobby, and went to a pay phone.

His partner Ross answered on the tenth ring.

"What is it?" Ross said.

Dave said, "We've got a problem."

"Tell me."

"Vannerson," Mayfield said. "He's gotten himself in trouble."

"Does it have to do with us?"

"No," Dave said. "But he could take it there. He's threatened to."

"Does he want more money?"

"No," Dave said, "he wants us to help him out."

"You mean work for him?"

"In a way."

"What do you think?"

"I think the man's threatening us."

After a while, Ross said, "Well, we can't have that."

Dave said, "No. I didn't think so either. I'll see you soon."

Thirty-One

The confrontation with Vannerson and the other cop had souped him up, and Kessler wondered if he should go straight home or stop someplace to get a drink. He decided against the drink, telling himself that wasn't the way to come down. He needed to be sober, needed to think.

He was driving on the Broken Arrow Expressway. He glanced at the speedometer and saw that he was going almost ninety miles per hour.

"Jesus," he said. He eased off the accelerator. He needed to calm down or these guys would have him killing himself.

But he couldn't take his mind off Vannerson. Or that bloodthirsty friend of his. Sitting there in a strip club, plotting his downfall.

He saw the Harvard exit and thought, Jamie. Swerved across two lanes, putting the car in a four-wheel skid for a couple of seconds, but hanging on and regaining control. Caught the downward ramp off the highway and turned left onto the road.

Jamie lay on the hotel bed clothed only in her T-shirt and panties. She had come to the hotel straight from Kessler's office and had not gone home to get her bathrobe. But it didn't matter. There was no one around to see her. To her surprise, she found it easy to relax. She ordered a club sandwich from room service and watched two movies. The first flick had Jodie Foster playing a woman who falls in love with a man sent to kill her, played by

Dennis Hopper. It didn't make much sense; there was zero chemistry between Hopper and Jodie Foster, and the actors playing the bad guys all seemed to be wishing they were in another movie. After that, she watched an old movie with Paul Newman and a very young Melanie Griffith, looking no more than sixteen and far too grown up even then. Paul Newman had gray hair in the film, maybe fifty at the time, but was sexy enough to keep Jamie's interest. Her mother had always loved Paul Newman. It was weird: in the movie, Newman looked a little bit like Sam Clay. Fiftyish, gray-haired, handsome. But there the resemblance ended. While the character—his mannerisms and personality—reminded her of Kessler. A little. Though he looked nothing like Paul Newman, she wondered if he thought he did. Well, that was often the problem with good-looking men. They were rarely as cool in real life as they were on screen. She clicked the television off when the movie ended, crawled under the blankets and went to sleep.

She awoke to the sound of knocks thumping on her door, scaring all holy hell out of her. Disoriented and terrified, thinking, *he's found me, the crazy bastard has found me,* until her scrambled senses discerned Kessler's voice saying, "It's me, Jamie. Paul Kessler. Open up. Please. Please, I have to talk to you."

She sat up in bed, saying, "What do you want?"

"I need to talk with you."

She knew he was not dangerous. She knew it and she sensed it. She said, "I'm not dressed."

"Well, get dressed," Kessler said. "And let me in."

She got out of the bed, wrapped the blanket around her waist and opened the door.

He came in quickly, looking very spooked, and shut the door behind him.

Jamie said, "What's the matter?"

"What's the matter is your buddy Van," Kessler said. "He's trying to frame me for murder."

"That's crazy," Jamie said. "Van wouldn't do that."

"Yeah," Kessler said, "how do you know that? Just how well do you know this fucker?"

"What is the matter with you?"

"Did you tell me everything? Huh? Did you tell me everything about Greg Vannerson? Or was it just the part that helped you?"

"I don't know what you're talking about."

"Did he send you to me?"

"What?"

"Answer me, goddammit. Did he send you to me?"

"No," she said. "No. Why would you think that?"

"What?"

Jamie said, "Why would you think that?"

Kessler stopped and processed her question. Why *would* he think that? . . . If she hadn't told him about Vannerson, he wouldn't have gone to Cassy's. Wouldn't have found Monty and followed him out to Turley. Wouldn't have seen Van. Would probably be going to jail in the morning.

"Paul . . . ?"

Kessler sat down on the bed. "I don't know," he said. "I don't know why I'd think that. . . . I'm sorry."

She sat on the other bed, across from his. "What's going on?"

Kessler said, "I saw him tonight. He had driven Carol's car north of the city."

"You saw him drive her car?"

"No."

"Then how—"

"I just know. Okay?"

". . . Okay."

After a few moments, Kessler said, "This man you say is a 'pretty good guy,' how well do you know him?"

"I don't know, he . . . he's always been nice to me."

"Is that it?"

"He's not a murderer. He's not a bad person."

"How do you know?"

"I don't know, nobody knows that sort of—"

"Are you in love with him?"

"No," she said, like the suggestion was idiotic. "What is with you?"

"Why are you defending him?"

"Look, I'm not defending him. . . . All right, maybe I am." She said, "Listen, he said he would try to help me, and I think he did."

"On Wednesday night, you mean?" Kessler said, "When you asked him to talk to Sam?"

"Yes."

"Did you ever speak to him about it since? Ever say, 'How did your talk with Sam go?' "

"No."

"And you believe he really would try to help you?"

"Yes. I do."

And if he had, Kessler thought, he would have seen Sam that night. Maybe before Sam killed Carol, maybe after. And then he had been drawn into it. Maybe that's what this whole stupid mess was about. Just bad timing, bad luck. And it had led to this. Christ.

Kessler lay back on the bed and looked at the ceiling. "Maybe he was," he said, almost to himself.

Jamie said, "What?"

"Maybe he was trying to help you."

"Yeah, maybe . . ." And then the sight of him touched Jamie somehow. She said, "Are you all right?"

"No," Kessler said. "I'm not all right. I feel like I'm in a war zone."

She looked at him for a long time, as he continued to stare at the ceiling. Then she climbed onto the bed with him, let the blanket drop off as she kneeled next to him. She bent over him and kissed him on the cheek, and then the other cheek. Then kissed him on the mouth.

Kessler said, "Jamie . . . what are you doing?"

"Don't talk," she said.

". . . Jamie . . ."

"Don't talk," she said. "Think of a wall . . ."

Thirty-Two

He left her hotel room at two-thirty in the morning. It was not that she had asked him to leave—she hadn't asked him to leave or stay—rather, it was a stubborn determination not to be chased out of his own house. He was not going to let these people do that to him. At two-forty-five, he pulled the Buick up into his driveway and turned off the ignition.

Then the interior of the car flooded with light.

A car had pulled in behind him.

Kessler opened the glove compartment and took out the .38 snubnose revolver—the same one the cop had stolen from him days ago. He opened the car door and pointed the gun into the glare of the headlights.

"Paul, *Paul*. It's me, Hank."

Hank stepped out of the car and Kessler lowered the gun. "Jesus, Hank, you scared me." Kessler put the gun in his jacket pocket. "What are you doing here?"

Hank turned off the car's ignition. The headlights died. "Your car," Hank said. "Remember?"

Kessler looked at the BMW behind the Buick. The new one that they had agreed Hank would pick up in Dallas. He could not tell it from the one that was now sitting on a farm in Alva, holding DNA like a petri dish. It was identical. It was perfect.

Kessler said, "Did you switch the VIN numbers?"

"Yeah," Hank said. "And the model numbers too. In this light, you can't tell the difference at all. In good light, you can. I mean, *you* can, because you're familiar with the old one. But if you weren't, you wouldn't."

"That's great," Kessler said. "How much?"

"Fifteen, including delivery." Hank said, "Good thing you just won a case."

"Well, that's less than what I'd have to pay Marty to defend me at trial."

Hank handed him the keys. He said, "Listen, I've gotta go. You gonna be all right?"

"I'm fine," Kessler said. "You need a ride home?"

"No, Bobbie's here." Hank pointed to a Dodge pickup idling in the street.

Kessler studied the man and briefly wondered if it was the late hour or the recent unexpected sex that was making him emotional. Mostly, he thought of Hank having just spent the last twelve hours on the road, retrieving this car, saving his ass.

"Hank . . . listen, I don't know how to—"

But Hank was already walking down the driveway. "Forget it. You'll be fine. Get some sleep." And then he was in the truck and then he was gone.

Kessler stood in the driveway, counting his blessings. Then thinking: and I almost shot him.

He unlocked the front door of his house and walked in. Buddy hit him on the back of the head with his nightstick, using a descending arc, and Kessler went down, unconscious before he hit the floor.

Thirty-Three

The trunk of the BMW opened and Kessler made out the faces of Vannerson and Matlock, Vannerson smiling. Then Buddy turned on his flashlight and shined it into his face and he couldn't see again. His hands were in front of him, bound together with duct tape. They hadn't used their handcuffs on him. But he didn't find it that unusual. They probably used handcuffs on the people they put in police cars, not the ones they stuffed in car trunks. No handcuffs, no police car—two very bad signs off the bat. They weren't in uniform either.

Buddy said, "I swear, this boy is going out of his way to help us. I knocked him out and what did I find? His car keys in one pocket, fucking gun in the other. You'd think he'd've been smart enough to get rid of this gun, since he knows we took it from him already."

Buddy held the .38 aloft in a plastic bag. There was a shotgun in his other hand. He poked the barrel of the shotgun into Kessler's chest. "You took it off Ray, didn't you?"

Kessler said, "It didn't belong to him."

Buddy said, "You killed him."

"I didn't kill anyone," Kessler said. "What happened to your friend was an accident. You want to blame someone, blame the man who sent him after me."

And then Van spoke. "Paul, why don't you knock off the divide and conquer shit. It ain't gonna sell. Buddy trusts me, I trust him. Okay?"

Kessler said, "So you sent Miller after me?"

"Of course I sent him," Van said. "I'm his lieutenant. If Buddy takes issue with that, he knows he can talk to me about it. I don't expect you to understand that." Van made a gesture. "So, you bought a substitute car. How did you know you couldn't wash the DNA out of the old one?"

"I watch a lot of 'Law & Order,' " Kessler said.

"Well," Van said, smiling, "I got to tell you, it was a pretty good idea. It probably would've worked. Those homicide dicks, they're not as smart as the guys you see on television."

Kessler said, "They've never managed to catch up with you, have they."

"No," Van said. "They have not." Proud of it, apparently.

Lying in the trunk of his own car, Kessler said, "Well, are you guys gonna read me my rights?"

Van laughed at that one. "Man, you've got balls. Get him out, Buddy."

Buddy handed the shotgun and the .38 to Van and grabbed Kessler by his jacket and pulled him out. Kessler lost his balance and fell on the ground, and Buddy kicked him twice in the side, saying, "Get up, *get up.*"

"Easy, Buddy," Van said. "We're not animals."

Buddy looked at Van, wondering if he was serious and then saw that he was. So, reluctantly, he helped Kessler to his feet. Kessler was grateful for Van's small measure of compassion, though, in part, he was as mystified by it as Buddy.

Van handed the shotgun back to Buddy and took Kessler by the arm. "Come with me for a minute," Van said. "I want to talk to you."

They walked away from Buddy. They got a few feet when Kessler heard Buddy rack the slide of the Mossberg shotgun, putting a round in the chamber. He tensed for a few awful moments, waiting for the blast to hit him in the back. It didn't and he realized that the other cop was still standing next to him.

Kessler relaxed, a little. He took in his surroundings. They were on a dirt road in the country. There was a good deal of brush next to the road and a forest in the distance. The terrain was not flat, and Kessler wondered if they were in Osage Hills.

Van said, "Don't mind Officer Matlock. He tends to get a little too . . . enthused about the work sometimes. Besides, right or wrong, he holds you responsible for the death of Officer Miller."

"I told you," Kessler said, "it was—"

"I know," Van said, "it was an accident. I believe you. Listen, I've been a police officer for a long time. I understand people. You're no killer. I know that."

"You know?"

"Yeah," Van said. "I know. I want you to understand, this is nothing personal."

Kessler held up his bound hands. "Maybe not to you," he said.

"Ah, I wish you could understand," Van said. "We're not . . . wicked people. We have reasons for this. You said it yourself: this isn't about you. It's just . . . circumstances."

"Circumstances?"

"Yeah."

Kessler said, "You mean, like a war?"

"Right."

Kessler said, "Why tell me that?"

"Because it's important to me," Van said. "I want you to know that this has nothing to do with you dissing me at Cassy's. I wouldn't do that."

"You wouldn't do what?"

"I wouldn't kill a man because he talked smack to me. I'm not as small as that."

In the midst of this terrifying situation, it dawned on Kessler that this had to be one of the strangest conversations he'd ever had. He wondered if the guy was dinking with him. Then he hoped the guy *was* dinking with him, because if he wasn't, it meant he was crazy. Dispensing moral philosophy to a man he intended to kill. Seeking . . . what? Respect?

Kessler said, "If the end is the same, what difference does it make?"

Van said, "It makes a difference."

"You draw distinctions?"

"Of course. Don't you?"

"No," Kessler said, "not like this."

"You don't understand."

"I understand very well. You're a man of pride and you want to convince me you're not a fucking criminal. But you're wasting your time."

Van frowned. "Man, you don't make it easy on yourself, do you?"

"You're wrong about that," Kessler said. "Did you kill Carol?"

"No. Sam killed her."

"Then what's the problem? Look, whatever you're into, I don't care. It's not my business. So why don't you just leave me out of it?"

"You know I can't do that," Van said. "If Sam goes down, he'll take me down with him. You said it yourself."

"Okay, I said that," Kessler said. "But I said it because you were coming after me. Trying to frame me, trying to kill me. And, funny as it may seem, I *do* take that personally. Leave me alone and you've got nothing to worry about."

Van said, "It's too late for that."

A car was coming down the road. It came to a halt, scrunching dirt and gravel. A man got out.

It was Sam Clay.

THIRTY-FOUR

Van brought Kessler up to Clay so that they were standing a few feet apart. Buddy stood off to the side, still holding the shotgun.

"What's going on?" the chief said. "What's he doing here?"

Van said, "I thought you might want to say something to him."

"What the hell would I want to say to him?"

Kessler didn't know either, but he didn't feel like keeping quiet. So he said, "You might tell me why you killed Carol."

That got his attention.

"What?" the chief said. "Who the hell are you to ask me that? You fuck my wife and you accuse me of murdering her? And now you question me? Who are you?"

Kessler eyed him steadily, then said in a low voice, "Sam, who are you trying to convince now? It's just us out here."

Chief Clay punched Kessler in the face. It knocked him down.

"You son of a bitch slime," the chief said. "How dare you? How dare you? You rotten son of a bitch scumbag. You've got no sense of decency. You had no right to do that. No right."

Kessler wiped some blood from his mouth. "You're right," he said. "I didn't. It was my sin. But you shouldn't have punished her for it. Not that way."

"What I did with my wife is my business."

"But you've made it my business," Kessler said. "You sent these men to kill me. To frame me."

225

"You're goddamn right I did," the chief said. "What are you going to do about it, you piece of shit?"

"He might sue you, chief," Buddy said, and Van laughed, though the chief didn't. Kessler stood up.

"You're just a punk," the chief said. "You're a nobody. You don't know anything about my world. The real world."

Van had been watching this exchange and he decided now that the time was ripe. "Chief," he said, "this guy's making things too difficult. He's making up lies about you, spreading stories to the press. He keeps talking about people trying to frame him, but he's the one trying to frame you. There's no question about it. Now I don't like bringing him out here for this, but I don't see any other way. It's got to be done."

It took a moment for it to sink in and then the chief said, "You mean you want me to . . . ?"

"Yeah."

"Here? Now?"

"Yeah," Van said. "Here. Now."

The chief said, "Are you serious?"

"Yeah," Van said. "It's the only way."

The chief said, "You mean just shoot him?"

"Yeah," Van said. "You've got your service weapon."

The chief looked at Van and then at Buddy and then at Kessler. And then back at Van.

"I don't know, Van."

"What's the problem?" Van said.

"I mean, we haven't planned this thing out," the chief said. "You can't just call me out here in the middle of the night and spring this on me."

Van said, "I did it for you."

"Now wait a minute," the chief said, "I didn't call you in the middle of the night—"

"No," Van said, "you wait a minute. I sent a man after this

guy to kill him. For you. And that man is dead now. He died trying to save your ass. And now you've got an opportunity to take care of it yourself, and you're gonna say no?"

The chief said, "Van, it's not that easy. I shoot him now and the shot will be heard."

"No," Van said, shaking his head, "the nearest residence is five miles. There's nobody around to hear anything."

The chief looked at his gun, but he didn't touch it.

Then Buddy said to Van, "I told you."

"What?" the chief said, sounding more defensive by the minute.

Van said, "You've never drawn your service weapon in your life, have you?"

"What are you talking about?" the chief said. "I've been a police officer for almost twenty-five years."

"Yep," Van said. "And now you'll never get to draw your pension."

And then Van shot Sam Clay three times in the chest with the .38.

It happened that quickly. Kessler was just thinking, *no*, when Van made the comment about the pension. *He didn't mean . . .* And then it was done. And Sam Clay lay dead not ten feet in front of him.

Van moved past Kessler and crouched down next to the chief. Buddy came up and stood just behind Kessler.

"Is he dead?" Buddy said.

Van said, "Yeah."

Kessler saw Van use his eyes to communicate something to Matlock. What it was, he didn't know exactly. But he understood the basic premise of it. He heard Buddy step away from him and he turned to see Buddy walking back to his car, confident that Van had the situation under control.

Kessler turned back to look at Van.

Van had not yet reached for the chief's service weapon, so Kessler realized he still had a chance. Van was still squatting, examining Clay's body, maybe looking for a recording device.

Kessler said, "Thanks."

Van looked up at him, curious. "For what?"

"For saving my life," Kessler said. "He was about to shoot me."

Van said, "Is that what you—"

He didn't get to finish the sentence because Kessler kicked him full in the face. Van cried out as the force of it knocked him on his side and Kessler stepped in and kicked him three more times, a couple of blows to the kidneys, hard as he could do it, and then another solid one to the face, and he heard the man groan and then there was the sound of Buddy in the distance, saying something, and Kessler bent over with the idea of taking Clay's service weapon, but it was wrapped tightly in a holster, so he picked up the .38 that was lying next to Van and ran, as he heard Buddy shouting at him, yelling, "Hey!", but he kept going, past the chief's car and starting to round it as the first shotgun blast came, slamming buckshot against the car, and then he was in the brush, alive and running to the dark comfort of the woods, which opened up and took him in, as he heard another blast . . .

Buddy lowered the shotgun. He stood behind the chief's car and peered into the darkness. He turned to look at Van. Van was still on the ground. Buddy looked to the woods again and then back to Van. "Are you all right?" he said.

Van's voice sounded almost like a moan. "No . . . I think my nose is broken . . . *go get him.*"

Buddy looked back to the woods. They were about seventy yards away. Seventy yards of brush to cross before he reached the woods.

Buddy said, "Has he got a gun?"

Van said, ". . . What?"

"Did he pick up a gun?"

"I don't know."

Buddy looked at Van again, tentative. "The .38," Buddy said, "where is it?"

"I don't know," Van said. "He must have taken it."

A five-shot snubnose, Buddy thought. Two shots left. No match for his shotgun and a Glock .40 with ten in the clip.

But goddamn, there was a lot of open ground between here and the woods.

That was why Buddy decided to speak up.

It turned out to be a mistake.

THIRTY-FIVE

Kessler hid behind a boulder, catching his breath. The woods were dark and deep all right, but they weren't that inviting. He couldn't see ten feet in front of him. It was a moonless night and the only light to be had was in the brush he'd just run across. He could see out of the woods, but not into them. So he crouched behind the boulder and thought about what he should do.

If he kept running, there was a good possibility he'd trip over something and fall. There were no well-beaten paths in this damn forest. None that he could see, anyway. If he tripped and fell, he might break something. Then there would be nothing left to do but wait for one of them to walk up and shoot him. If he fell, he might smack his head on a rock and do their job for them. He had to weigh it. He couldn't panic, because if he did, they'd get him for sure. He just needed to sit here and think. Just for a couple of seconds.

Then he heard Buddy call out to him.

"Kessler."

The voice was distant. Buddy was not in the woods. He wasn't too close.

"Kessler."

Kessler peered over the rock. Through the trees, he could see Matlock. He wasn't even in the brush. He was still behind the chief's car. The shotgun lying across the trunk.

Buddy spoke again, "Kessler. Come on out. We're not going

to kill you. Just come on out of there."

Kessler thought, like hell I will. Guy must be off his rocker.

"Come on out of there," Buddy said. "There's not going to be any more shooting."

Or he was a goddamn fool, Kessler thought. Or he thought Kessler was one, if he was going to fall for this line of shit. *Oh, there's not going to be any more shooting? Well, dagnab it, why didn't you say so?* Stupid prick.

And then Kessler thought, no, he's not stupid. He's frightened.

He's frightened too.

He's frightened because he's human.

He's frightened because he's a man.

Kessler raised his voice to speak. "I'm staying here."

Silence.

Moments ticked by.

Then Kessler saw the flashlight come on, and he ducked down behind the boulder. The light passed over the woods, illuminating the area behind him. He hadn't been seen.

Buddy said, "You don't come out of there, I'm coming in."

Kessler kept quiet.

Buddy said, "You hear me? I'm coming in there!"

Kessler leaned against the rock and pointed the gun towards Buddy. He was still behind the car, still way out of range, but he could walk into it if he wanted. It was up to him. Kessler steadied himself and then said it so they could both hear it.

"Buddy. You're okay where you are. But if you come back here, I will point this gun at your chest and I will pull the trigger."

"Hah!" Buddy said, "You're so full of shit you're gonna float out of those woods."

"Do whatever you want to do, Buddy. It's your choice."

"You're gonna shoot *me,"* Buddy said. "I'd like to *see* that."

Kessler decided he'd said enough.

A long minute passed as Buddy Matlock stared at the woods and they stared back at him, and he waited for the lawyer to say something else, maybe plead for his life or say something stupid and desperate like, "We can make a deal." Or, "I mean it."

But nothing else came. There was nothing else. No sound but the wind.

Buddy continued staring. A few more moments passed.

And then he turned to Van. "If I had a rifle . . ."

"Oh, Jesus Christ," Van said. "You've got a shotgun."

Buddy said, "That's for close range. He's a good sixty yards away."

"Then move closer."

"Van, that goes completely against training. I walk across that field and I'm exposed."

"Well, what the fuck do you want me to do? Call in the tactical team? You know we can't do that."

"I can't get a clear shot at him from here," Buddy said. "I can't even see him."

"I don't believe this," Van said.

"What are you mad at me for? You're the one he took down."

"Well, where were you?"

"You told me to—"

"Never mind," Van said. "Listen, he's got two shots. You draw one of them out and the flash will tell you where he is."

"Draw it out? Where? Into my belly?" Buddy looked at Sam Clay's dead body. He said, "I don't even know what I'm doing here."

"Dammit, Buddy, if he gets away, we're fucked. Don't you get that?"

Buddy took that in. Then said, "Maybe if we both go."

Van was thinking he needed to go to the hospital. His nose was broken and he was afraid he might be bleeding internally where Kessler had kicked him in the body. His head felt like it was full of broken glass. But he raised himself to his knees, and then to his feet. Then he reached out to steady himself against the car. He felt dizzy. Almost faint.

"Give me a minute," he said.

"Van . . ." Buddy said, uncertain.

"Just a minute," Van said. "And then we'll both go after him. You and me."

They walked out past the car and spread apart about twenty feet. Van shined his flashlight on the trees, back and forth, back and forth, but didn't spot a man to shoot at.

Buddy walked slowly, both hands on the shotgun.

They reached the halfway mark and slowed their pace. And then they moved closer, fifteen yards, and closing. The dark wall of forest began to lift and they could discern the shapes and forms of the trees.

Van wished that Ray Miller were here. He was a country boy, a hunter from the Piney Woods. He'd feel right at home in this situation, tracking prey. They could use a backwoodsman now.

They drew to the edge of the woods and exchanged glances.

Van said, "Paul?"

No response.

"*Paul.*"

Nothing.

"Paul. Why don't you come out of there? It's over."

Van motioned to Buddy to move farther down. The men spread farther apart and then went into the woods. Buddy held his shotgun with one hand and his flashlight in the other. Noisily, they waded farther in, their beams waving about like lasers. They were too far apart to talk to each other now, though each could hear the other's movements and took some comfort in them.

They needed the K-9 unit, Buddy thought. Dogs to flush the

son of a bitch out. But Van would say that was not possible either.

Buddy heard Van call something out which he couldn't understand. So he yelled out, "What?"

". . . seen anything?"

"No."

"Keep going, then."

Well, no shit, Buddy thought. Van didn't sound so good. He didn't seem to be thinking too clearly either. If Buddy had seen something, wouldn't Van be the first to know? Like he'd find the lawyer and decide to keep it a secret. It worried him, Van being in that state.

Buddy continued the search and had just begun to fear the guy had doubled back to his car when he heard a voice. Not a shout or a panicked cry. But something almost conversational. Cold. "Hey," the man said. And Buddy whirled to see the man sitting on the ground, pointing a gun at him, and Buddy moved, trying to keep the flashlight in his hand while bringing both hands to the shotgun to steady it and fire, and Kessler shot him in the chest.

Then shot him again.

It socked him hard, twice, and he felt himself stagger back, paralyzed by it. He dropped the Mossberg, the life coming out of him by the second, and he sat down, as things got remote and dark and quiet. He tasted something in his mouth which he vaguely thought was blood. He wanted to get up, but he couldn't . . . He was aware of the ground beneath him, wet and a little cold . . . And then he was aware of the lawyer standing over him . . . holding the Mossberg now, saying something to him, like he was mad at him for something. It seemed funny, that. Funny that the lawyer should be the one that was angry.

Kessler said, "I told you."

Told me? What . . . ? . . .

When he heard the shots, Van's fear was that they were .38s. They had that sound. He thought, Paul? And then he waited for the third shot. The third shot would show that they were not .38s, but .40 calibers shot out of Buddy's service Glock.

He waited ten, twenty, and then thirty seconds.

But there was no third shot.

Oh, God.

He stood where he was and called out. "Buddy!"

He thought he'd seen Buddy's flashlight a second ago. But now was extinguished and there was only darkness. And quiet. So much quiet.

"Buddy! You okay?" Jesus, two cracks from a .38. And then nothing.

"Buddy!"

Van thought, maybe they weren't .38s. Maybe it was Buddy's Glock, shooting at nothing. Panic shots . . .

Then he heard Paul call out to him.

"He's dead, Van," Kessler said. "I'm sorry."

Van heard the words and thought his head would split. He could hear Paul's voice, distant. But he couldn't see him. It couldn't be, Van thought. The guy was just a lawyer. A civilian. It wasn't in him to do it.

"What have you done?" he said. "Goddamn you, what have you done?"

Kessler thought, I got lucky. But he could talk about that later. He said, "Van, I've got a shotgun and a Glock pistol. I don't want to use them. Let's call it a night." Kessler said, "Okay?"

"You're a murderer!" Van yelled. "You lowlife son of a bitch! You just killed a cop! You'll burn for this. Do you hear me!"

Kessler said, "Van, just go. Go home. Please."

"You'll burn! There won't be a trial. You worthless fuck cop killer! You'll see how it works. You're a dead man! You hear me! Dead!"

Van began to walk toward the sound of Kessler's voice and stumbled. He lay on the ground, sobbing helplessly, exhausted and distraught. He cried out, "You're dead!"

Approximately fifty yards away, Kessler racked the slide on the Glock and put it in his jacket pocket. Then picked up the shotgun. He left the flashlight off.

Slowly, Van got back up. Then began picking his way out of the forest. He made his way back to the clearing and to his car. The darkness was lifting; the sun would be up soon. He got into his Crown Vic and left.

THIRTY-SIX

He persuaded himself not to go to the hospital. It would complicate things. The ER staff would ask him what happened, and he would have to lie. If he told the truth, the place would be swarming with detectives and OSBI agents within minutes. He wasn't ready for that. He needed time to put it together, time to frame the right story. Time to think about what questions they would ask and how he would answer them. Time to rest.

When the time to talk did come, he would tell them that Kessler shot Chief Clay in cold blood. Then shot Patrol Officer Buddy Matlock. And then blindsided him.

No . . . That wouldn't work. Kessler would have had to have blindsided him first, then shot Buddy. After he shot the chief.

But then how did Officer Matlock end up in the woods, almost a quarter-mile away?

Well . . .

And what were you doing while Officer Matlock was trying to apprehend this criminal?

And, come to think of it, why didn't you call in the tactical team? Why didn't you call for backup?

It wasn't going to be easy, explaining it. If it got too complicated, he might have to scrap the notion that he was there altogether. Which meant he'd have to take care of the lawyer on his own. Or get a couple of friends to help him.

Maybe that wouldn't be so difficult. The guy was a cop killer after all.

He was relieved to see that his driveway was empty. Then he remembered: T.J. had a wrestling tournament in Midwest City. He and his mother wouldn't return until tonight. He wouldn't have to explain his condition to his wife. Not today anyway. It was a positive sign.

He had to stop at the front door and steady himself again as a wave of nausea swept over him. He held on and told himself that it was nothing to be overly concerned about. Maybe he wasn't bleeding internally. Maybe he was just tired. It was morning now. Another day. Sleep for an hour, get cleaned up, and put things in order. The lawyer wasn't going anywhere. He was too stupid to run.

He made it into the living room and took off his gun belt. He put his service weapon on top of the bookshelf. Then he walked into the kitchen.

"You don't look so good, Van."

Dave Mayfield was sitting at the table. On the table, near his right hand, was a .38 Colt automatic with a long silencer attached to it.

After a moment, Van said, "I had a rough night."

Dave said, "You look like you need to see a doctor."

"I'll be all right."

"Pardon my rudeness, coming in your home like this."

Van waited for something more. An explanation. He didn't get one.

Dave said, "Why don't you sit down? Let's talk for a minute. Then maybe we'll get you to a hospital."

Van sat down and took in the gun. He kept it pretty cool, under the circumstances. He said, "Dave, I hope you're not thinking of shooting me or something. Cop killers always get executed. Sometimes by other cops."

Van waited for the bullshit rejoinder. Who, me? Something like that.

But Dave gently pulled the gun closer toward him and, like that, it was in his hand.

"I've thought about that," Dave said. "I have. Kill a cop and you're likely to set off a vendetta. That's what happens. Normally." The gun seemed to be pointed now. Mayfield said, "But then, you're not a normal cop, Van. You're a crook. A gangster. Like me. You may not realize it, but you left your world behind long ago. And stepped into mine. Only, I don't think you've ever really understood that. And that's the real problem. See, over on this side, we have rules too. They're not the same as yours, but they're there and we have to respect them. You know what I'm saying?"

"No," Van said. "I don't know what you're saying."

"Come on, Van. You remember what happened to Marcus."

"What about him?"

"He was a good boy. But he was a rat," Dave said. "Like you."

"What the hell are you talking about?" Van said. "I never ratted you out."

"No, you didn't," Dave said. "But you threatened to. And in my jurisdiction, it's the same thing."

Van said, "Dave, I think you misunderstood me—"

But Mayfield went on as if he hadn't heard him. "You're really not a bad person, Van. Not really. You might have made a decent crook. Or a decent cop. But you can't really be both, can you? You can't really . . . mix it. You know what I'm saying? It's like serving two masters." Dave said, "Ah, listen to me. Giving lectures."

Dave Mayfield shot Van twice in the body, knocking him back off his chair. Then he walked around the table, bent over and put another bullet in Van's head.

Dave unscrewed the silencer from the gun barrel and put the parts in his jacket pockets. Then he walked out the back door.

THIRTY-SEVEN

Jim Kessler thought the OSBI agent sounded like an interesting guy and he wanted to know more about him. He said, "Do you think he believed you?"

Paul Kessler said, "I don't know. He was one of those smart guys, acts like he's a farm hand. Scared the shit out of me. I'm glad Martin was there."

"Did you lie to him?"

"I left some things out," Kessler said. Like smashing in the window of Carol's Volvo, dumping her body in Grand Lake, killing a cop . . . Jesus. "He was in a tough position, politically. He might have had to recommend charges if not for the woman. Jamie. I think he believed everything she told him. About the chief, about Vannerson."

They were in Jim Kessler's kitchen, sitting at the table drinking coffee. A few days had passed since the madness, and the Tulsa media had not yet determined Kessler senior's telephone number.

Jim said, "She still working at that place?"

Kessler shook his head. "No one is," he said. "The owner closed it down."

"They after him now?"

"I don't know," Kessler said. Or care.

"What about her, then?" Jim said. "Didn't you tell me she had a kid?"

"She interviewed yesterday with a friend of mine," Kessler

241

said. "Glenn Wheatley. He's a comp lawyer who needs someone. He called me afterwards and told me he was going to offer her the job. I think she'll like it there."

Jim said, "A law firm?"

"Yeah, I know. Another house of ill repute," Kessler said. "She's a good woman, Dad. She kept me out of jail."

There was a pause between them. Then Jim said, "You going to stay here a few days?"

"Tonight," Kessler said. "After that, I don't know."

Jim said, "You feel ashamed?"

Kessler said, "No." And meant it.

"You want to tell a priest?"

Kessler looked at his father, puzzled. He had never considered him religious. His mother had been the spiritual one. Maybe Jim thought her faith had passed down to him. Looking at his father now, a part of him regretted that it hadn't.

"I told you," Kessler said. "I had to tell somebody."

"Paul, the man walked into those woods to kill you. Even after you warned him." Jim Kessler said, "It's that simple."

"You think so?"

"I do," Jim said. "Believe it."

Kessler decided he would.

ABOUT THE AUTHOR

James Patrick Hunt was born in Surrey, England in 1964. In 1972, he and his family relocated to Ponca City, Oklahoma. He graduated from Saint Louis University in 1986 with a degree in aerospace engineering, and from Marquette University Law School in 1992. He practiced law for approximately thirteen years and for much of that time he represented police officers on matters of civil rights and labor arbitration. He is the author of *Maitland* and *Maitland Under Siege*.